Dedi

This book is dedicated to my Grandpa Andrew Lovett whose love for me never came short. Who possessed a quality of compassion that held great rareness. To My Grandmother Sarah Lovett whose kindness and love for others inspired me to want to inspire others and touch them how she touched many. For giving me life lessons like "Manners will take you where money won't." It took me all of my 17 years to finally realize what that quote actually meant. To My Uncle Lamont B. Lovett only we know the bond we share, just know I'll forever be proud of you and I love you. To the rest of my aunts and uncles Danielle, Jessica, Adriane, Karsheem, Papa and Raymond I love you guys more than you'll ever know. To my big sister Crystal even though I wish you were here to celebrate this with me I know where you are there's no suffering I love and miss you. To my Granny Earline Jackson I miss you and love you dearly and I know you're looking down on me telling me to reach for the stars. To my Steppie Ronnie Rowson thank you for loving me like your own and always treating me like your "Baby girl" and not like your step child. For loving me so deeply. To my Daddy William Nedd thank you for being supportive. To Marcella, Simone and Sheridan I'd never imagined our bond to be as unbreakable as it is today we aren't friends we're sisters and love y'all so much. To save the best for last to my Mommy, my best friend and my everything words can't explain how blessed I am to have a mother like you. When I first told you about this endeavor you said you'd be behind me a thousand and ten percent. Not many get a mother like you and I promise to cherish you forever and ever you're my heart and I love you.

To my beautiful curvy girls never forget your worth and unique beauty. Be proud of who you are no matter how many times society judges you, you are beautiful.

Graciously Flawed

Kai N.

Graciously Flawed

Copyright © 2015 by Kai N.

<u>Published by Kai N. Publishing</u>

Fresh Start

Kelsey

My body is something I've never really embraced until I realized how much of a rare beauty it was. No, it wasn't that perfect coke bottle shape, but it was beautiful to me and that's all that mattered. It took a while for me to appreciate my curves but now that I do I feel unstoppable, beautiful and most of all, perfect. The question is, will I ever find someone that feels the same?

I woke up feeling good, there's no specific reason why, I just felt calm and on top of the world. You'd think I'd be annoyed to go back to school especially after the bomb ass summer I just had, but I felt the total opposite.

I was ready to walk the halls of Chadrich again and show my new look. In the months prior, I focused solely on reinventing myself. I wasn't in dire need of a makeover but it was time to change it up and that's just what I wanted to do.

I looked over my body admiring its many curves. The outfit I decided to wear accentuated my voluptuous figure. The hip hugging boyfriend jeans showed my round bottom and the white tank showcased my full chest. I needed to calm this down a little bit so I grabbed my sheer Kimono and draped it around my arms.

"Perfect!" I thought to myself.

"Kelsey, come down!" my mother's voice echoed throughout our home.

"I'm coming!" I yelled back.

I unwrapped my hair, gave myself another once over and headed downstairs

I could hear the throwback R&B playing and I already knew my mother was in a good mood, it's probably because my father was coming home from business.

I shook my head as I watched her wave the spatula up and down as she swayed her hips to the beat.

"Ma, what's wrong with you?" I said through laughter, she turned around and smiled widely.

"Girl I was about to tear it up, you don't even know!" I shook my head and sat at the breakfast bar.

"So are you excited?" she asked, I took a sip from my orange juice.

"Surprisingly I am." I looked down at my phone and then back at her.

"I can tell." She put some eggs on a plate and handed it to me.

"How?" I asked, putting a forkful of eggs in my mouth.

"You look happy baby." She caressed my cheek and then took a sip from her coffee mug.

"When's Daddy coming home?" I asked.

"Tonight." she beamed.

"How'd the trip go? Did they grant him approval?"

"The mayor of Atlanta loved the idea of the state of the art indoor Football field."

I smiled brightly.

My father happened to be one of the most successful African-American Architectures in the world and I'm not over exaggerating. He was featured in Forbes top 100 and has designed buildings everywhere. Even though he's successful his business sometimes interferes with home life. With him being so fortunate he sometimes has to put business first and I'd be lying if I said I didn't miss him but he's grinding so we can live comfortably so I try my best to get over it. I looked down at my phone, checking the time.

"Mom, I have to go so I don't be late, thank you for breakfast." I kissed her cheek and walked out of the door. I walked towards my car, a silver Range Rover. It was a congratulatory gift from my parents after getting accepted into the National Honors Society. I remember walking into the driveway and nearly passing out after seeing the beautiful shiny silver exterior. A bright pink bow adorned the hood; just thinking about it puts a smile on my face. Lord, I wonder what my graduation gift is going to be.

Mid-way to school I got a text from Aria. Aria and I have been best friends since the beginning of freshman year; it was almost like we meshed automatically. She was me and I was she.

"Can you come pick me up?" she asked through sniffles. I sighed lightly. I should be nervous but unfortunately I'm not. I knew those cries oh so well and I knew the person who created those tears was her boyfriend Christian. If I tell you how much I dislike that boy you'd be surprised.

Let's start by saying he's in his second year of college. Besides him being old as hell, he's always broke and is always saying something to mentally break Aria down. As many times as I want to just slap her and say leave him I can't, my job is just to be there for her.

"I'm on my way." I hung up and made a detour to her home. She lived maybe 10 minutes away from me so I got there in no time. She got in on the passenger's side. Her eyes were red and puffy from crying.

"What did he do now?" I asked.

"He butt-dialed me and I heard everything from the beginning to the end." she sniffled. "And when I called him back pissed he had the nerve to call me an insecure, immature bitch! I cursed him out and hung up. Now he's sending me crazy messages and he won't just leave me alone." She looked out of the window and then back at me.

"Aria, he's not good for you and you just need to face that. After today, leave it alone. You need someone who's going to value you and he's not the one."

She nodded and turned to face me. "You're right, I love you Kelsey." She leaned in to hug me but stopped and looked me over.

"Girl, are you wearing make-up?" she asked. I laughed.

"Yeah I did a little something." She smiled.

"Who are *you* looking cute for?" she asked.

"Me, myself and I." I grinned.

"Excuse me." She pulled a compact mirror from her purse and checked her makeup. She cleaned some of it up because it had begun to run from her crying. She added some more mascara and then flipped her hair.

She went back into bad chick mode in 2.0 seconds. If anything Aria never stayed down for long. She bounced back quickly.

"Are you good, are you okay?" I asked her once more just for clarification.

"Yeah, the best thing for me to do is to not think about him and I'll be fine." I nodded and focused my attention back on the road.

"Are you ready for Prom and stuff?" I asked her.

"Yeah, I'm ready to be done with high school more than anything though,"

"Me too, I still can't believe it though. This time next year I'll be in a dorm somewhere."

I sat at the red light and processed what I had just said. I've spent all four years of high school without a boyfriend, "boo thing" or let alone a texting buddy. I wrapped myself up in my school work as a way of avoiding my reality.

No one wants to face that they've been alone during the prime of their years, that's depressing. Hopefully it'll be different this year, maybe a higher spirit's been holding back on my special someone for this long, maybe I'll get him this year.

All of A Sudden

Kelsey

The stares were beginning to wear on me, all day people were looking trying to figure out if I was a new student or not. Four whole years of walking down these halls and I'm barely known, I had allowed myself to fade into the background.

If that didn't make me feel bad, the whispering did. All day every time my name was read off of the attendance roster, the whispering began.

"Damn, she look good bro, I wonder how she did it."

"I wonder what waist trainer she uses."

"Damn, that can't be Kelsey Washington."

"She look good for a big girl."

Every comment pissed me off more than the last, how could people talk like their ignorance couldn't be heard?

"Psst," the poking of a finger forced me to turn around.

When I did, regret set in almost instantly. I was trying to figure out why Imani, the same Imani who never cracked her teeth to me once before, the same Imani who's in every boy's face in this school, wanted to ask me anything.

"Girl, what hair do you buy?" she smacked her gum loudly while a mischievous grin covered her face

"It's my hair," I said simply and turned around.

Even though I had a couple of pieces in she didn't need to know that. Before she could say anything else the bell rang. I grabbed my bag and gladly exited. Aria stood in front of the door waiting for me.

"So let me tell you what happened in 2nd period!" I turned to face her.

"Drama already?" I asked.

"Let me tell you the tea," she yelled dramatically. The closer we got to my locker, the more animated she got. I couldn't help but laugh. All of her talking fell on death ears after I spotted the finest specimen known to man *Calvin Powers* leaning on my locker.

He's every girl's weakness here at Chadrich, and secretly he was mine too. He stood at 6ft. 7in. with beautiful brown skin, his body was conditioned to play the hardest of sports and his short curly haircut gave him a male model look, not to mention he could dress his ass off. And he was standing next to my locker. I was about to get an opportunity to utter just a few words to him and that freaked me out. What if I say the wrong thing? Or crack a corny joke I can't recover from? What if?

Many times I fantasized about being with him, standing under his tall stature. Too bad, he's never paid me any attention. I mean he complimented me once but that was only on my sneakers, so it doesn't count.

Standing next to him was Dwayne. He was another one of

Chadrich's finest looking boys. Like Calvin, he played football and was known for having had a notorious crush on Aria like none other. They dated for exactly 2 weeks before they broke up. Aria likes to say it's because of his immaturity, but I think it's because of her boyfriend Christian.

"Oh God, look at thing 1 and thing 2." she rolled her eyes and pulled out her cellphone

Calvin was leaning on my locker while Dwayne's eyes stayed focused on Aria. The closer I got to Calvin, the more I could smell his intoxicating scent. I mean, God could he not be any more perfect.

I watched his every movement while silently surveying his body. Though he was fully clothed you could still see the outline of his toned body. You could tell he had a serious workout regimen.

After minutes of staring at him, I finally gained enough courage to speak.

"Excuse me." I said, softly. He turned to face me and I watched as his hazel colored eyes surveyed my plush body. His thick tongue ran over his perfectly pink plump lips.

"My bad." He moved over giving me space to get to my locker

With every turn of my lock, I could feel him burning a hole in the side of my face.

"36," I kept repeating to myself. I sucked my teeth

This cannot be happening right now. After all the times I've had to mess up on my locker, now had to be the time?

"Let me help you," he offered, the deep raspy texture of his voice did something to me. If I wasn't about to pass out earlier I'm definitely about to now.

Instead of him allowing me to move over so he could help me he came directly behind me and stood extremely close.

I was frozen in place. I watched as his long arms reached around me and landed on my lock.

I know I shouldn't be allowing him this close into my personal space but I couldn't move and quite frankly I'm not sure I wanted to.

"What's your code, Ma?" I cleared my throat,

"I don't just give out my code to anyone." I said with a little bit more attitude than intended.

"I'm not just anyone, besides I don't steal. Now what's your code?" I could feel my cheeks heat up almost instantly.

"13, 4, 36." I watched as his fingers turned the dial and tugged on the lock slightly.

"See, was that hard?" he asked, his lips were inches away from my ear.

His cockiness and straight forward attitude was a turn on to me.

Dwayne, if you don't back up!" I could hear Aria's voice throughout the hallway interrupting me and Calvin little moment. I don't know where Dwayne and she disappeared too.

Calvin's hands fell to the side of him but he stayed right behind me.

"Girl, stop acting like you don't want this!" she groaned and rolled her eyes. She then turned her attention to Calvin and me.

The look of annoyance disappeared and a smile formed.

"What y'all was over here doing?" she asked.

"Calvin was helping me with my locker, that's all." I said

answering her.

"Umm-hum," she side eyed me. When I turned to face Calvin I noticed his eyes were glued to my backside. He lifted his head with quickness when he noticed I caught him.

"Thanks again for my locker," I said trying to get rid of the sexual distraction that just took place.

"It's no problem Ma. Just like that he walked away his minty breath still lingering in my nostrils.

"So what did I miss? Y'all looked pretty cozy to me," she asked.

"Nothing girl, I told you he was just helping me with my locker." I grabbed my bag and put it on my arm.

"Yeah whatever, I'll find out sooner or later. Let's go eat for now though." I nodded and walked with her.

I'm still trying to figure out myself what that was and why all of a sudden he's taking so much interest in me? Is this God's way of giving me what I've been longing for?

"I'm just saying Aria, why now? Why all of a sudden is he acting that way towards me?" I nibbled on the pizza I decided to buy for lunch.

"Girl, have you seen yourself? He's just finally making a move." She took a sip from her smoothie.

"What do you mean, finally?" I asked.

"He's probably had his eyes on you for a while now, I don't know. All I know is the way he was staring it looked like he has been scoping you out for a minute."

I scrunched my face up and shook my head. I must've been

blind because interest is something I've never seen in his eyes.

"Whatever! Enough about me what about you and Dwayne? Where did y'all run off to?" I asked trying to change the subject.

"*I* went to my locker and he followed behind me talking nonsense."

"What do you mean nonsense?" I asked.

"He was telling me that I should stop playing and give him a chance and that he's not the same immature little boy he used to be." She pushed the pasta around her plate.

"Well, why don't you give him a chance?"

She rolled her eyes and looked my way. "I'm good on all of that, besides I have Christian."

You'd think after him treating her the way he did she'd leave him. But in all actuality, I knew she wasn't. It would take a lot more for her to leave. I just remained quiet and ate the rest of my food.

"You ready, we can't be too late going back." I said.

"Yeah, let's go." While we were leaving the Pizzeria, I could see Calvin leaning on his G wagon. While we were at my locker I wasn't really focused on his outfit because I was trying to gather my own thoughts. Let me tell you now that I got to savor the moment and I definitely did.

I took all of it in, from the dark Balmain jeans and crisp white Bathing Ape t-shirt all the way down to his white Rick Owens. His style was so original and his confidence was out the roof He didn't need to be cocky for anyone to know that.

"Kelsey stop staring, he's coming over here." Aria nudged me.

Just as those words left her lips, I could see Calvin walking towards me. Even his walk was perfect. God, why was he so gorgeous?

"Wassup y'all?" he spoke coolly.

"Hey." Aria and I said at the same time.

"Can I talk to your friend for a minute?" he asked Aria.

"Sure, give me your keys so I can go sit in the car." I turned to face her and handed her my keys while mouthing "Oh my God." She blew me a kiss and walked off.

"A Range, huh?" Calvin asked while looking down at my keys.

"Yep," I said trying to shade my nervousness.

"You don't have to be like that around me," he said while smiling and displaying those beautiful dimples.

"Like what?" I asked.

"Nervous, I know I'm cute and it can sometimes cause nervousness but baby there's no reason to be." I rolled my eyes and laughed lightly.

"If anything you should be nervous around me, I'm the cute one."

I'm not sure where this burst of confidence was stemming from but it was showing out and if I wasn't mistaking it looked like Calvin was enjoying every moment of my sassy attitude.

"Damn Ma, here I thought you were so quiet and innocent." he said through a smile.

"I'm not quiet, I just choose who and who not to speak to." I said.

"Oh really? So all this time you were choosing not to speak to

16

me?" he asked.

"Not even, you've never spoken to me so..." I trailed off.

"Well, let's change that then, when you see me speak." I leaned back a bit shifting my weight to my right foot.

"Are you asking or telling me?" I questioned.

"What does it sound like to you?" He gave me a sly smile.

"Hmm, I'll think about it." I smirked and walked ahead of him, switching my hips in the process.

Admiration

Calvin

I watched as Kelsey walked around the gym, her plump ass in those leggings caught the eyes of half of my team members. After I helped her at her locker a couple of days ago, it was almost like I couldn't stop thinking about her.

"Yo, what y'all think about Kelsey?" I asked.

A group of us sat around the water coolers struggling to catch our breaths. Those laps around the gym can tire you quickly.

"She cool, why?" Bradford, one of my teammates, asked.

"I'm trying to holler at her," I said seriously. It was true I saw something in her I've never seen in any other girl.

"I mean she pretty, just a little too thick."

I looked at him and turned my head sideways. "Too thick? There's no such thing as *too thick*." I said.

He looked at me and laughed. "I'm just saying, I like my girls with a small waist and thick ass. If they're light skin, that's even better."

"Have you seen your mother? She's five feet, dark skin and definitely thick."

"Damn!" my teammates yelled while laughing.

"You went too far," Bradford said while getting up and going to the locker room. He was such a sensitive ass.

I never understood why young boys had that ignorant ass concept lodged so deeply in their brain. Then again, they were boys; men have real mature views on a woman. A man looks past the surface and deeper inside. I may be young but my pops put me on as soon as I was old enough to talk.

"Alright, get y'all asses up and run those laps!" Coach yelled.

I hopped up and stretched my legs while catching a quick glimpse of Kelsey. She was talking to one of the girls standing next to her. It wasn't who she was normally with. I knew that much.

I jogged over towards where she was standing. She was so deep into her conversation that she didn't notice how hard I was staring. I mean it was like I couldn't take my eyes off of her. She had something a lot of these females in Chadrich didn't, and that was class. Her name never came up when my boys and I were talking about which girls we smashed. She was never the topic of conversation, she was never in drama and her grades reflected what kind of person she was. Shorty's beyond bad. Who in their right mind wouldn't wife her up?

"Yo bro, let's go before Coach bugs out." Dwayne slapped my back and kept jogging ahead of me.

Running was the last thing on my mind. I was focused on how I could approach her without sounding like these corny ass dudes she was used too. I'm not sure how I'm going to do it, but I needed to figure it out and soon.

New Thing

Kelsey

"My favorite classic would have to be *Lean On Me*." I bit into my French fry.

"Nah it was cool, but I like comedies better so I'm going to go with *Coming to America*." Calvin said, slumping down in his seat with one arm draped around the seat next to him.

Calvin and I's topic of conversation often varied. It could go from entertainment and fashion to politics in a split second and that's what I love.

"Boy you need to take a second look at life, *Lean On Me* was extremely inspirational.

We both laughed as I took a sip of my milkshake.

"Let me taste it," he reached for my cup but I pulled it back.

"Uh-uh! I told you to get this and you said no, so you're not getting anything."

"Oh really, not even after I paid for it?" he smirked.

"Nope, goodbye." He poked his bottom lip out.

"Fine, here." I pushed the cup towards him.

He smiled lightly and I rolled my eyes in annoyance. He scrunched his face up and passed the cup my way.

"That shit's nasty."

I rolled my eyes. "No one told you to drink it, greedy." I snatched my cup and began to sip from it.

"This is my song." I whispered as Brandy and Monica's "The Boy Is Mine" played throughout Shake Shack.

It's been a couple of months since Calvin and I's first interaction and I must admit our friendship has grown into something I couldn't ever imagine it being. He's everything I've pictured him to be. He was a complete gentleman in every aspect.

From September to now, he's convinced me to go to lunch with him. While on these small friendly dates, my infatuation with him has grown. Too bad he's never once made a move. The most he's ever done was compliment me on how well I carry myself or how dope my outfit is.

I moved my hips to the beat and sung along to the song that was playing. Calvin's eyes were dead set on my actions. I didn't care though, I was having a moment. I playfully hunched my shoulders and watched as Calvin's lips curved into a smile, showing off those perfect dimples. His smile faded a bit but his eyes stayed fixated on me.

I began to grow a little uncomfortable under his stare. "What?" I asked.

"Yo, why are you single?" he asked. His elbows were on the table and he was hunched over, waiting for a response.

That question took me completely off guard. I was stuck for a minute trying to figure out how I was going to answer that question. I couldn't say I don't have a boyfriend because no one has ever shown interest in me. I just answered the halfhearted truth.

"That's a great question, a question I can't answer."

I bit my lip trying to figure out what to say next. He was adamant and ready for an answer so my small little answer wasn't going to cut it, nope not today. The way he looked at me it was like he wanted me to elaborate, but I wasn't too keen on going that far.

"I'm choosing to focus on school." I looked away and took another sip of my milkshake. It was almost like he could see right through me. He moved his lips to the side and gave me a pointed look.

"Come on Ma, be real and honest." He leaned forward while I sat my milkshake down on the wooden table.

"Fine, I really don't know why I'm single. I've been single for so long I never thought on the topic that much, but why are you asking?" I asked. I was now curious as to why that was rattling his brain so much.

"To be honest Kelsey, you're beyond beautiful. You're so classy and shit; you have what a lot of girls our age don't. Aside from your looks, you're practically a genius. Any dude who had the chance to wife you up and didn't is beyond stupid. If I had the chance to make you mine I'd-" He stopped.

I took a huge gulp. I was not prepared for whatever he was about to say next.

"Never mind." He just smiled and looked down at his watch. "We should get going, so we don't be late." He grabbed our trash and dumped it.

I could sense he was holding something from me. After hanging around Calvin for these couple of months, I've noticed how honest he is. He's an open book and doesn't dare to hold back an opinion. I know whatever he didn't say now, he'd say eventually.

When we got back to our school, it was almost like I didn't want to leave him. Being around him practically made my day so much that I looked forward to seeing him every day. I looked forward to every text we exchanged and every lunch we spent together. He just has that effect on me.

"Damn, I can't even get a hug? I took your ass out and everything."

I giggled lightly.

Calvin stood in front me with his arms outstretched waiting for me to fall into them. Instead I sighed, pretending to be annoyed.

"Oh word?" He stood there with a fake pout. I couldn't help but laugh at his silliness.

I walked towards him and wrapped my arms around his muscular body. He smelled amazing, like a mixture of a manly cologne and a fresh bar of soap. I could fall asleep just from the scent.

His arms wrapped around my waist securely and a feeling I couldn't describe ran through me and as cliché as this may sound the butterflies in my stomach were running rampant.

"Call me, ugly." He pulled away but his hands kept a firm grip on my lower back.

"I will."

He moved his lips to the side. "You say that all the time and my phone never rings, so stop lying."

"I promise I will." At this point, there was no use in trying to hide my chocolate cheeks that were now rosy red. Before I could move away, he kissed my forehead softly and walked away.

There was something about those forehead kisses that just triggered something in me, especially when the lips are as soft and delicate as Calvin's.

I walked in the classroom with a smile not even the devil could wipe off. I searched the classroom for Aria. She is normally the first one here if we aren't together so it was strange to not see her. A few minutes later, she came strolling in. She, too, had a smile on her face, a smile I hadn't seen in a while.

She placed her bag in the spare seat next to her and pulled out her notebook as if she didn't have some tea of her own to spill. She could sense that I was staring at her so she turned her head.

"What?" she asked, acting clueless.

"You know what, why are cheesing so damn hard?" I asked.

"The same reason your ass is." Her grin expanded.

"I'm not sure what you're talking about, can you elaborate?" I said sarcastically.

"I saw you and Calvin pull up in the school's parking lot." She smiled slyly.

"And the only way you could've seen where I was is if you were in the parking lot too, so care to share?" I said returning her sly attitude.

"Girl! Let me tell you!" After holding it in for so long, she was beyond ready to share and I was ready to listen.

"Tell me." I egged her on.

"Well after you and Calvin left, Dwayne and I decided to link up and go out for lunch."

I tilted my head and opened my eyes widely. "You and Dwayne? Lunch?" I asked, surprised.

Aria had made it no secret how annoying she felt Dwayne was so to hear that they had lunch and both of them came back not only unscathed, but happy as well, surprised the hell out of me.

"Honestly Kelsey, he's a great person and I can recognize his maturity. Not to mention, I was laughing the entire time. I just wish I wasn't as bitchy towards him as I was, but things have changed and so has my attitude."

Aria and Christian's relationship was complicated to say the least, but it seemed like Aria was pulling herself further and further away from him. I can't lie and say I'm not happy to see her pulling away. I just know it won't be as easy to get rid of him as she thinks it is.

"So what about you and Calvin?" She bumped me with her elbow.

I paused for a minute trying to gather my thoughts. Just thinking about him puts me in a calm and peaceful place.

"Look at you, you're freaking blushing!" she said loudly.

"Shh! Stop being so loud, we're going to get in trouble." I whispered.

She waved her hand dismissing what I said. "Who cares, just say it already." She leaned in looking so intrigued.

"Nothing too crazy. He was just asking me questions, questions that had me thinking."

"Hello Miss, can you tell me more? I need details." She moved her hands in a circular motion.

"He just asked me why was I single an-"

"Ladies in the back, stop the talking!" Mrs. Colbey scolded us.

We rolled our eyes and whispered low.

"He was saying how beautiful and smart I am. Then he started to say something along the lines of if I was his, but he stopped." She sucked her teeth.

"See that's exactly what I hate, like can you just talk?" She rolled her eyes.

"I know that's basically it though, I do feel he's hol-"

I was cut off by Mrs. Colby's presence. "Ladies, class is over in 5 minutes. Can you be quiet until then?"

Aria and I nodded and just sat quietly for the remainder of the class. *What an eventful day*, I thought to myself.

Prepared For My Parents

Kelsey

I could always tell when my father was home early from work. *ESPN* was always blaring through the house.

"Daddy!" I yelled.

"I'm upstairs, babygirl."

I put my bag on the sofa and walked up the stairs towards his office.

My father, even after all of these years, still managed to look not a day over 20. His muscular build and tall frame was enough to scare off any young boy, and I'm sure he enjoyed having that quality. Overprotective was an understatement when it came down to my dad. His motto was, "No dating until 60 and no children until 70." Yeah it may have been a bit excessive but I thought it was cute to say the least.

I walked towards his desk and kissed his cheek lightly. "How was your day, Dad?" I sat at the edge of his desk while his eyes stayed buried deep into his paperwork.

"It was okay; I got a lot done before my trip to Chicago."

I sucked my teeth and rolled my eyes.

"Don't start princess." He spoke sternly.

"But Daddy, you just got back from Houston and then you

were in Atlanta before that. When are you going to be able to just stay home and relax?"

"When I retire." He laughed lightly. My father always used laughing as a way to escape from my actual feelings, especially when it came down to him working.

"Come on Dad, I'm serious."

"Kelsey, do you not like the house we live in? Do you not like the car you drive or the clothes you wear? The only way I can give you those things is if I work for it."

"Fine Dad." I just dropped it to avoid any lectures.

"Don't be like that, now what time is it?" he asked

"It's almost four, why?"

He hopped up and grabbed his hoodie off of the couch next to the door. "Shit. We have to go meet your mother at the shop!"

Like my father, my mother is an entrepreneur. She owns one of the best hair salons in the Tri state area. My parents are a true and honest power couple.

"Dad, why'd we take the truck? Why couldn't we take the Porsche or something? You know it's too hard for me to get in, I'm way too short." He put on his seatbelt and turned on the radio.

"You'll be fine drama queen, now put on your seatbelt." He waited until I did so and then pulled off.

As soon as we entered the salon the endless chatter came to an end. My father was a hot commodity at my mother's salon; women, young and old, fell over him.

"Hey Lathan," they all cooed.

I rolled my eyes and walked towards my mother's station.

Seeing as though she wasn't there, I sat down in her styling chair and pulled my phone out. Unfortunately like many of the teenagers my age, I was addicted to social media. I scrolled through my timeline, occasionally double-tapping a few pictures that were mainly of celebrities.

As I continued to scroll through my TL, one picture caught me completely off guard. There Calvin was with his arm wrapped around a girl. I couldn't deny her beauty. Hell, a blind man could see how beautiful she was.

Her wild curly mane sat almost perfectly on her shoulders and her beautiful light skin had a slight sun kissed effect to it. Calvin's lips were pressed against her cheek while she gave the camera a silly face. I could feel my heart practically fall out of my chest after reading the caption that followed beneath.

@calvinpowers_ *"My princess is leaving me to go back to college. I'm going to miss her annoying ass."* #lovethisgirl

College, how could I compete with an older girl? She practically matched him perfectly. She looked like an athlete and his type. I knew it was too good to be true. All of my fantasizing was just that a fantasy, a fantasy that would never become reality.

I couldn't be angry with Calvin though. I'm nothing more than a friend and vice versa.   Instead of pondering, I just got off of it. I clicked out of the app and stuck my phone in my back pocket.

"Kelsey, if you don't get your ass out of my chair, you're going to get it!" My mother yelled dramatically.

As odd as this may sound, I loved to hear my mother curse, it was the funniest thing. Sometimes I did things just to purposely annoy her and just to hear her rant.

"Lord Mommy, why such violence?" I slapped my hand against my chest and gasped.

"Get your dramatic ass away from me." She couldn't help but laugh at me.

"How was your day?" I leaned in and kissed her cheek lightly.

"It was pretty good, what about you? How was school?" she asked while unplugging her curling irons.

"It was good, pretty uneventful." I began to pick at my nails.

"And Calvin?" she asked a little too loudly.

My mother and Aria were the only two people who knew about my crush on Calvin.

"Mom, not too loud. I don't want Daddy to hear you."

She smiled, "Your father's here?" she asked.

"Yep, I left him up there with Mrs. Esther." We both giggled.

You always come across that one older person who has zero cares in the world and Mrs. Esther was that person all the way. She'd openly flirt with my dad and every other man who entered the shop, but that was just her way and it was harmless.

"Oh Lord, and you never answered me. How's Calvin?"

"He's cool." I didn't want to tell her what I just found out because I didn't want to think on it.

"That's good, that's good. Let's go rescue your daddy, though. I think he's suffered enough." We both laughed and walked towards the waiting area.

"You know what, Lathan? If I wasn't married to Cleofus, I'd take you right from Liana." Mrs. Esther said to my father.

My mom and I stood off to the side listening in on what she was saying. I tried to contain my laughter, but once my father started to entertain her, I couldn't help but laugh. We walked closer towards the cluster of women.

"Mrs. Esther, what did I tell you about flirting with my husband?" My mother tried to cover up her smile.

While my mother and Ms. Esther playfully went back and forth, I noticed how hard my father was staring at my mom. He was looking at her like she was a piece of gold. My mother was on the curvy side and that's where I inherited my figure from. Unlike me, my mother didn't have as much as pudge as I did.

"Hey honey." My father got up and pulled my mother towards him. He kissed her sweetly and then complimented her on how good she looked. I must admit, my mother was always dressed to die for.

The royal blue wrap dress matched her suede royal blue Louboutin heels perfectly.

I watched as they held each-other close. If I could have love like this at least once, I'd be content and satisfied with life.

Under Cover Feelings

Kelsey

I sat on the cold bleachers shaking my legs up and down from the cold air that kept blowing.

Today I promised Calvin that I'd come to his game and boy did I pick the wrong day. It was 43 degrees and freezing wasn't even the word. I zipped my jacket up and blew into my hands, hoping to gain any warmth.

Luckily the game was close to being over so I just had to stick it through. With every glance Calvin threw my way I shielded my uncomfortable feelings. I was afraid of hurting his feelings or seeming like I was uninterested.

Chadrich was leading, of course, thanks to Calvin and Dwayne's quick footwork.

"Girl, look at Dwayne's butt. It's like the most perfect little muscular cakes I've ever seen!" Aria squealed. I looked over at her and meshed my eyebrows together.

"I'm sorry boo, I just can't help it." She flipped her hair.

Unlike Calvin and I, Aria and Dwayne's relationship surpassed platonic. They'd been getting pretty serious and cute was the only word to describe them. There was one minute left and Dwayne was running towards the end zone.

In a swift motion, the football was in Calvin's hands and he was leading the team to victory. We cheered him on as he made it to the end zone in record time.

I'm not sure if I was cheering because we won or because I was finally going to be out of this cold. Aria and I got up and walked towards the field, but before I could get there a tap on my shoulder forced me to turn around.

"Wassup Kayla," he stuffed his hands in his pockets and looked me up and down.

"It's Kelsey." I corrected him.

"Oh yeah, my bad. I just wanted to say hey." I stood there soaking in the awkwardness.

"Well hey," I waved and then looked away. He parted his lips to speak but before he could say another word, I was lifted off of my feet from behind and hoisted in the air. I automatically noticed it was Calvin due to the tattoos that covered his arms.

"Calvin, put me down. You're sweaty!" I screamed.

Everyone looked in our direction, including a couple of unhappy ladies. He finally put me down and when he did I noticed Tate was gone.

"What did he want?" Calvin asked, referring to Tate.

I hunched my shoulders. "I'm not sure" I straightened my clothes.

"Yeah, well stay away from that dude, he's no good." I rolled my eyes.

"Calvin, you are not my daddy." I walked ahead of him only to be pulled back by my waist.

"Keep playing," he whispered in my ear. Calvin's overprotective attitude really started to increase after our friendship began to grow.

"Whatever." I rolled my eyes playfully.

"But you saw me out there, I was killing." He did a little dance and then threw his arm around my shoulder.

"You were okay; don't let anyone hype you up." I said while smirking.

"That's strike two, keep playing and that ass will get left." He said sternly.

I rolled my eyes.

Calvin just loved threatening to leave me even though he wouldn't dare. He knew better.

"Boy bye, I'm going to the bathroom." I fanned him off and walked ahead of him.

"Alright, meet me in front of the school when you're done."

I nodded.

I stood in front of the sink while the warm water ran over my hands. I could hear the toilet flush and a stall door open up. I looked through the mirror to see who it was and there stood Imani. I mentally shook my head at her outfit of choice.

Imani was known for her promiscuous ways and she loved to embrace it. As sad as it may seem, I feel she's taken pride in it. The cropped top she wore fell inches below her breast and the tight white skirt she wore stopped just above her knee. I can't lie and say she isn't beautiful because she truly is. It was just her actions that overshadowed her beauty.

"Hey girl." Her voice just oozed fakeness.

"Hello." I knew I sounded uninterested and that was just what I was going for. Imani wasn't my friend nor a person I wanted to have a newfound friendship with. Many people may say I'm judgmental but if you would've known how bad she talked about me in the past, you'll understand my strong amount of dislike for her.

"Kelsey, right?" she asked.

I nodded she knew exactly who I was but I was going to play along with her little game. "Yep." I grabbed a paper towel and dried my hands.

"Calvin's friend, right?"

I turned to face her. "Yep, that's my friend." I leaned on the edge of the sink, waiting for whatever she was about to say next. I was slightly amused by her curiosity. All she was trying to do was figure us out so she could make her next move.

"He's so fine, isn't he?"

"Yeah, I guess." I pulled my phone out and began to text Calvin telling him I'll be out soon.

"Well can you do me a favor?" she asked.

I arched my eyebrow. "What's that?" I asked.

"Tell him to text me." She handed me a piece of paper with her number written on the front. I was so close to rolling my eyes and throwing it in the trash but I didn't want to give her the satisfaction of seeing me sweat.

I grabbed it and stuck it in my jacket pocket.

"Thanks girl." She smiled and walked out of the bathroom.

I rolled my eyes and looked in the mirror. "What does she

have that I don't?" I said, speaking to no one in particular. There was some times where I have a few insecure moments. I will admit it but just as quickly as they come, I shake it off and they seem to just fade away. I shook my head, grabbed my bag and walked out.

As soon as I reached the exit, I saw Calvin leaning on his G wagon engrossed in his phone. Even in a Nike jogging suit he managed to look good.

"You ready?" I asked.

He popped his head up from phone and looked in my direction.

"My fault, yeah let's go." He grabbed my purse and put it in the backseat along with his gym bag.

I sat in the passenger seat and he hopped in the driver's side. The cool air from the window being open blew in my face, causing my hair to blow back.

There was silence in the car. Nothing was on but the radio which wasn't normal, we'd be cracking up by now. I was annoyed by the whole thing with Imani; it had put me in my feelings.

"Yo, you good?" Calvin asked.

"Um-hum." I swiped my hair behind my ear and looked out the window. At night Jersey was so busy, it reminded me a lot of the city.

"Kelsey, why are you trying to lie to me? You know I hate that, be real and tell me what's wrong."

"I'm fine, but before I forget, here." I reached in my jacket pocket and handed him the small piece of paper that Imani had given me in the bathroom.

He stopped at the red light and grabbed the paper out of my hand. He scrunched his face up in confusion. His face changed from confusion and quickly turned amused. His laughter began to fill up the car.

"What's so funny?" I asked with an attitude.

"You, aww, you're jealous?" he questioned while poking my cheek. I swatted his hand away. On the inside I wanted to slap him for being right and knowing me so well.

"Boy, get your hands out of my face and don't flatter yourself." I folded my arms across my chest and slumped down in the seat a bit.

"Yeah, whatever. The only reason you have an attitude right now is because you know I'm right!" He rolled his window down and threw the paper out.

"What did you do that for?" I asked.

"That girl is not my type; you should know that by now. Besides, I have my eyes on something much more beautiful." I could feel his eyes burning into the side of my face.

It was something about when he stares at me. The level of intensity is out of the roof and I can sometimes feel myself growing nervous under his glare, like right now.

I looked out of the window as a way of shielding my nervousness. I rubbed the back of my neck and fidgeted with my fingers.

I watched as the scenery changed, the city lights weren't as bright and the stores were minimal.

"Calvin, where are we going? This most definitely isn't the

way to my house."

"You'll see Ma, just relax and enjoy the ride." I looked over at him and shook it off. I trust him so I'm sure I'm good.

We rode as the artist Partynextdoor played throughout the car. Although I was curious as to where we were going I was enjoying the ride, especially because Calvin was beside me. I'd occasionally glance over to the side of me. I watched Calvin focus on the road. I had come to realize that when Calvin was really focused, I mean really focused, he'd furrow his eyebrows or bite at his lip.

We began to slow down and I perked up a bit. I looked around for signs or something, but the place was completely bare.

"Calvin, where are we?" He ignored me and opened his door. I scrunched my face up and watched as he jogged around to my side.

"Hello, I'm talking to you." I waved my hand in his face and he finally looked up at me and smirked.

He hovered over me and our lips were inches apart. His cool minty breath blew onto me as he spoke. "Why can't you just chill and follow me, huh?" His deep voice made everything sound so sultry.

"I'm I-" The words were caught in my throat and no matter how many times I cleared my throat the words just wouldn't come out, he had officially shut me up.

"Come on." He put his hand out for me to grab. As soon as our hands met, it was almost like an electric volt shot through the both of us. He looked up at me and then back at our hands. Things like this only happened in movies and the romance novels I read. I believed none of this happened in real life but it did and it was happening to me.

We finally got out of the car and almost automatically Calvin's hands covered my eyes. His body was pressed up behind mine and the heat was almost too much for me.

"You good?" he asked.

"Besides the fact that I'm completely blind in the middle of nowhere, I'm fine." I said sarcastically. I could hear him chuckle lightly.

"Man, be quiet and step up." I did as he asked. I could hear the faint sound of opening credits to a movie.

"I'm serious Calvin; I'm in the middle of west bubba-"

He uncovered my eyes and I couldn't help but gasp. I fell into his chest and covered my eyes. A small park was where he brought me and what covered the park was enough to bring me to tears.

Lean On Me was playing on a huge projector screen and a whole set up of candles, flowers and a blanket sat on the ground. Beside those things, a plethora of my favorite snacks sat in a clear bag.

"Oh my God." I whispered. The tears begin to run down my cheeks.

"Why are you crying?" Calvin asked sincerely.

I was overwhelmed with emotion. This had caught me completely off guard.

"All of this for me?" I asked as I looked over at the layout in front of me.

"Yeah, and if a couple of flowers and a movie makes you react this way then I'll do this all the time." He said smoothly.

I turned to face him. "Why me though? Why'd you do this for me?" I asked trying to make myself believe that this was actually happening.

"I'm about to be mad real with you right now." He paused and then sighed.

He continued. "Kelsey, this friendship shit is not cutting it for me. I want you and I've been wanting you for a minute now. This friendship is cool, but I want more. I know you felt that back there. I know you feel the chemistry. What I'm trying to say is I want you be my girl. I want you to be mine." I froze and at that moment everything flashed before my eyes.

Everything from the lunch dates and laughs we shared all the way down to the Instagram post with him and the unknown girl and my most recent interaction with Imani. I wanted so badly to say yes, but I just couldn't. So many thoughts were running through my mind. I couldn't make a choice, not right now.

"So what's it going to be?" Calvin grabbed both of my hands.

"I-I can't." I stumbled over my words, trying not only to convince Calvin, but convince myself as to why I said no. I looked up at his face and I couldn't really read whether it was disappointment or shock .I was about to explain myself until he cut me off.

"Listen, you don't have to explain it to me. That's your decision and I'm cool with it, I'll wait," he smiled lightly and I did the same. He stuffed his hands inside of his sweatpants and looked at me.

"You ready?" he asked.

I nodded and walked towards where the flowers were. I picked each of them up and then walked back to where Calvin was standing.

"You like them?" he asked.

"I love them." I smelled them and walked beside him, heading towards his car. "You know you wrong for that though?" he said.

I looked at him. "For what?" I asked.

"Making me look mad corny, you had me all the way out there looking like a punk," he joked and I smiled.

"It doesn't go unnoticed." I said sweetly.

He opened the door for me and I slid in with ease.

The ride to my house was silent; it wasn't an awkward silence though. I guess we were both trying to process what just happened.

"I'm guessing after today, no more morning pickups?" I said trying to lighten up the mood.

We both laughed lightly.

"Na', I'll be here at 7:45 to be exact, and don't have me waiting because I will-"

"Leave your ass I know, I know." I said, finishing his sentence. "Night Calvin, thanks."

"No problem, you know I got you."

I blushed lightly and then leaned over to kiss his cheek sweetly. I got out and walked towards my door. I fiddled with my key and then stuck it in the door. I turned around, waved to Calvin and then opened my door.

As soon as the door closed I face palmed myself.

"What in the hell was I thinking?" I groaned.

I looked around. Seeing as though all the lights were off, I assumed everyone was asleep but that wasn't the case.

There my mother sat, her legs were crossed and her head was wrapped in a bonnet.

"So you must think you're grown, coming in my damn house at eight on a school night!"

If it's not one thing, it's another.

Right Choice

Calvin

That whole thing with Kelsey has been weighing on my mind heavy. I tried talking to my boys but they don't understand. There was only one person who I can be real and honest with. My father's studio was the first place that came to mind. His record label had successfully taken off in 94', right before I was born. Since then, he's signed some of the most talented acts out here.

"Hey Pops." I walked into the small studio room and sat at the soundboard.

"Baby boy what's up, you're looking like me more and more." He dapped me up and then pulled me in for a hug.

My father and I share a bond that a lot of my friends and their fathers don't. He's dope, relatable and understands where I'm coming from.

"Nothing much, it's just that these last couple of days I've been stressing, Dad." I leaned back in the chair.

"What's going on; is it school or football?" he asked.

"No, it's about Kelsey." I told my father before how much I was feeling her and he told me to let her know, but not once did he tell me what to do if she said no.

"Did you tell her how you were feeling?"

"Yep, Pops I had a nice little set-up." I leaned forward and put my elbows on my knees.

"And what did she say?" He rubbed on his beard.

"No, she wasn't having it Dad." I shook my head.

"Damn she's a tough one, she reminds me of your mother. When I tell you your mother made me work for it, I had to work for it. I mean picking her up, dropping her off and even joining some whack ass debate team just to show I was willing. At first I was like you, I wanted her and I wanted her then. But then I realized that if I wanted her that bad, I'd have to wait and give her time." He turned to face the soundboard.

"So when do you think she'll say yes?" I asked.

"Soon, but like I said, give her time." I sat there soaking in everything he was saying. If there was one thing I didn't like, it was waiting. I'm impatient but I know I didn't have any other choice but to wait, as hard as it may be.

"Yeah man, I guess." I leaned back again and ran my hand over my head.

I pushed a small button, letting the music fill the room. I bopped my head to the beat. I looked over at my dad, whose eyes were closed. This truly was his passion, music was his first love. He'd hate to admit it, but it was the truth.

"Listen to this part." He turned up the volume and I waited for the banger, the part that was going set this song apart from his other dope ass songs.

"Yeah Dad! You did it with this one. Its mad dope."

He looked up at me and smiled. "You know how I do boy;

your pops is the shit."

I shook my head.

A lot of people may dislike my father, but they'd have to admit that he's a dope ass Producer, writer and manager. His work ethic is crazy and that's where I get my passion for football from. He told me at a young age that no matter what I decided to do, I better be the best. He made it clear that odds are already set against me because I'm a black man. Everyone would be watching and waiting for me to fail, it was my job to beat the odds.

The vibration from my phone shook me out of my thoughts. I looked at my screen and noticed it was a text from Kelsey.

'Can you meet me at the Starbucks on Milburn Ave?'

I texted her back with quickness.

'Sure I'll be there in a few.'

I slid my phone in my back pocket, grabbed my jacket and got up from the chair.

"Dad it sounds good, but I got to get going."

"That's fine; just don't come in too late. Your Grandparents are coming over." I nodded, dapped him up and left.

Kelsey

I sat in Starbucks attempting to study but I was failing miserably. I was doing everything but that. After what happened between Calvin and me a couple of weeks ago, that's all that's been going through my mind.

I found myself going on his Instagram and going through all of his pictures, even the ones from forever ago. After the day he asked me to be his I noticed the same girl in another one of his pictures and the caption stated that that was his big sister. After finding that out, I felt I didn't give him a fair shot. I was going off of assumptions and that isn't cool, so I had no choice but to meet up with him and talk about it.

'I'm close by'

I read the text and nervousness rushed over me. I ran my fingers through my loose curls and tucked a couple of strands behind my ears. I took out my compact mirror, checking to see if I looked good. I looked extremely casual, but cute nonetheless.

The grey sweat jumpsuit fit me well and the metallic gold Air Maxes complimented the overall outfit.

I gnawed at my bottom lip contemplating on what to say to him when he got here.

I wanted without a doubt to be in a relationship with Calvin. I was just afraid and guarded. Having a friendship is a lot different than being in a relationship. This was what I've been wanting for so long, the opportunity was right at my fingertips. I'm finally getting what I'd been asking for and here I was afraid.

Should I just be real and tell him I wanted to truly pursue a relationship with him and that I was scared to admit it? Or should I just continue on with the friendship? I tapped my fingers against the table and then looked out the window next to me. I noticed Calvin's G-wagon pull into the empty parking lot.

My nerves were uncontrollable and it was getting harder and harder for me to calm them. I watched as he hopped out, picking up his pants a bit. The denim on denim he decided to wear looked so good on him.

Damn he's fine, I must admit it. I watched as he walked towards the entrance but not before wiping off his Delano designed tan colored Timberlands. I watched him intently as I always do. He just never catches me staring because I always play it off or turn my head.

He scanned the small crowd looking for me. I waved and when I caught his attention, his lips curved into a smile. I shifted in my seat a bit, closing the SAT book that lay in front of me. He swaggered towards me, kissed my forehead and sat down in the chair across from me.

"So what's up?" he asked.

God, the moment of truth.

"Nothing much, how are you feeling?" I asked.

"I'm cool."

"That's good. Calvin, can I be honest with you?" I got right into it.

"Sure, I'm all ears." He leaned in resting his elbows on the table.

"Calvin, what you did for me was beautiful. I've never experienced anything like that before. You treated me so special and I'm still in shock. To be honest, that's all that's been on my mind these past couple of days. I can't help but feel like I made the wrong choice by turning you down, but you have to understand where I'm coming from. I'm scared Calvin an-"

"Why though?" he questioned, interrupting me.

"Let me finish. I'm not use to this. I'm not used to companionship or the sweet gestures. It's all new to me; it's a shock to know that someone like you even took interest in me. I want to be with you I truly do, but I can't help but be afraid of hurt and judgmental people. I see the way girls, even grown women look at you, how can I compete with that?" I questioned.

The entire time I was speaking, his eyes were piercing into mine. It was messing with my mind and my train of thought. Not to mention he kept licking and biting his lips while staring at me.

He grabbed my hand and kissed it gently. I looked down at my hand and then back up at him.

"Kelsey, the whole time you were talking all I heard was that you're afraid and that's understandable, Ma. You have to understand, I'm no basic dude. I'm not about to be all in your face telling you how much I want you and need you and then I dog you out, that's not me."

"And that's not what I'm saying; I'm just nervous that I'll get emotionally attached and then someone will come along and take you from me." I spoke truthfully.

"I'm not gullible or thirsty for any female but you. Fuck whoever tries to come in between, I'm yours just like your mines, so what's it going to be?" He said smoothly.

"I honestly want to say yes, but how do I know you're being real? How do I know you aren't just being a smooth talker?"

"Like I said before, that's not me. I can sit here today and tell you some bullshit ass lies or I can give you some real rawness and I've been known to say the truth."

I stared at him, searching his face for any sign of fakeness or lies but nothing seemed to show. "Calvin, I'm telling you right now I'm no toy and I'm not to be played with, neither is my hear-"

"I'm here pleading my case to you looking like a cornball. I'm doing shit I've never thought about doing before, and you're asking me if I'm being real? I wouldn't have spent my money or time on someone I'd mess over Kelsey." I could hear the hint of frustration in his voice.

"Calvin, you have to understand where I'm coming from. I can't just jump into this with you."

He sighed and ran his hands over his face. "I'm not sure what more I can say because obviously my words aren't getting through to you. All I can do from this point on is show you, so give me an opportunity to do so."

I looked at him for a second. "Fine."

I watched as his lips curved into the biggest smile I've ever seen. It gave me a full look at the gold bottoms he had in that glistened along with his pearly white teeth.

"So what does this mean Ma, you mine?"

I smiled and nodded. I could hear him let out a breath. "Good man, I was really running out of shit to say."

I shook my head and laughed lightly. After our laughter died down, we sat there just ogling over each other's presence.

"You ready?" he asked while breaking our stare down.

I nodded while grabbing my Latte and SAT book off the table.

"Walk in front of me." Calvin said in a low tone of voice.

I walked ahead of him while he stayed behind. He was probably trying to stare at my back side. That's one thing about Calvin, he made it no secret how much he appreciated my curves. Words may have never left his lips, but his eyes did all of the talking.

"Where you parked at?" He asked.

"Over there." I pointed in the direction of my car.

"Let me walk you." He insisted.

Calvin's chivalry was something I adored. There were not many guys who share the same compassion that he does for a lady.

I opened my car door and put my books in the passenger's seat all while my Latte still occupied my perfectly manicured hands. I turned to face Calvin whose eyes were dead set on my actions. His arm held the door open for me.

"Thank you." His deep voice was enough to make you crave him.

"For what?" I asked.

"Giving me a chance to show you, you made the right choice."

I smiled and ran my fingers along his cheek.

"No, thank you for reassuring me I made the right choice." He leaned in. His lips were inches away from mine. I could smell the cherry Chapstick that adorned his lips, we were that close.

"Can I get a kiss?" He asked.

I didn't get a chance to say yes or no before I could feel his warm lips on mine. He grabbed my chin gently and deepened the kiss, his tongue massaged mine. The taste of his Chapstick filled my taste buds as I wrapped my arms around his neck.

This is the moment I had been waiting for, my very first kiss. I must say it was magical. Kissing had always seemed to be an intimate moment that you don't share with just anyone. It's meant to be special and that's just what it was, special.

Calvin's arm stayed firmly around my waist, pulling me closer and closer to him while our heads bobbed back and forth. Passion filled the air and I felt it with every kiss. It was obvious that I had made the right choice.

We finally pulled away. We were so close that the air seemed to be non-existent and words were the furthest things from both of our minds. We said nothing as our eyes did all of the talking.

"C-call me when you get home, alright?" Calvin said, stumbling over his words.

I nodded and waited for him to open my door. "I surely will." I bit my lip lightly.

"One more for the road?" he asked.

I smiled and pulled his neck towards me. Those lips, God I can get so used to them. Better yet, I can get use to *this*, to *him*.

Approval

Calvin

"Chill babe, relax." I tried my best to calm Kelsey down but she was bugging.

"Calvin, you don't know my dad. He's crazy when it comes down to me."

"He'll love me, trust." I watched as she bit her nails and bounced her leg up and down. I grabbed her thigh and squeezed it lightly.

"How is it that I'm meeting your family for the first time and you're the one who's nervous, relax."

"I know, I know." She swiped her hair behind her ear and turned to face me.

"Let me get a good luck kiss." I said.

She leaned in pecked my lips quickly and then pulled away.

"Yo, what was that?" I asked.

"A kiss."

"No that wasn't, that whack ass little peck."

"The last thing my dad needs to see is you tonguing me down, you'll definitely be dead."

"Fine, but later those lips are mine."

She smiled and looked away. "Calvin let's go, please."

I smiled and nodded. "Fine let's go so I can wow my in laws."

She smiled and walked ahead of me.

"Why'd you wear them jeans knowing damn well I can't appreciate them like I really want to?" She smiled and switched a bit harder.

That's one thing I appreciated Kelsey for and that was her curves and her ability to show them, without overdoing it.

"Always fighting dirty," I stood next to her on the front steps of her home.

"Baby, I'm so nervous." She said with one hand on the doorknob.

"Calm down baby, it'll be great," I leaned forward and kissed her forehead.

She sighed and then finally opened the door.

"Mommy! Daddy!" She called out.

"The kitchen." They answered.

She looked back at me and then walked in the direction of her kitchen. I took in the appearance of her house and from the looks of it her parents had bank. There was a good ass smell coming from the kitchen and it was enough to make your mouth water.

We finally reached the kitchen and all of a sudden I felt nervous. I've been cooling since we got here, but now after seeing her dad I could feel my palms get sweaty.

"Mommy, Daddy, this is Calvin," Her pops was mad tall and looked only a few years older than us.

"Hi Calvin!" Her mother was the first to say anything while her pops stood behind her, mugging me.

"Hello Mrs. Washington." I leaned in and gave her a hug.

"Hi baby, I hear so much about you." I watched her nudge Kelsey's father.

"What's up son?" He gripped my shoulder tightly.

"Hey." I had to stop and clear my throat a little bit because of how tight he was grabbing my shoulder, "Hello Mr. Washington, how are you?" I asked.

"I'm good, how about we go down to the basement and let the ladies talk." I nodded and followed behind him.

The man cave set up he had was pretty dope. The leather couches and a huge flat screen took up the majority of the space.

"This is really nice, Mr. Washington," I complimented him.

"Thank you, come sit here." He tapped the top of the bar. I turned and started to walk towards him. He pulled a silver briefcase out and slammed it on the countertop. I jumped at the sound.

"So Calvin, you plan on going to college?" He popped the briefcase top open.

"Yeah, I mean yes sir," I cleared my throat and rubbed my sweaty palms on top of my pants.

"That's good, that's good. Now Calvin," I watched as he pulled the silver colored steel from out of the briefcase he had put on the bar top. I swallowed a gulp and then sat up. I already knew this dude was no joke.

"Are you nervous Calvin?" He asked.

"A little Sir."

He lightly chuckled, "That's good. I want you to remember this time of you being nervous because if I ever find out you hurt my baby girl that feeling will return, understand?"

I nodded.

"Good, other than that, you seem like a good boy. I trust you now, let's go eat." All I seemed to be able to do is nod. He scared the shit out of me I can't lie, but I get it. That's his baby girl. If I ever have a daughter as beautiful as Kelsey, I'd act the same way. I'd play no games.

We got up and walked back into the kitchen. Kelsey was stirring a pot, giving me a full view of her round ass. One eye was on her ass and the other was on her Pops. I didn't want to die, so I diverted my attention.

"Calvin and Kelsey, can you guys go set the table?"

I nodded.

"Sure Mommy." Kelsey grabbed the forks and knives while I grabbed the plates.

As soon as we sat down to eat her mom's started firing questions at me left in right nowhere near as intense as her pops but it wasn't easy. She eventually let up and I was able to enjoy each of their company.

"Thank you so much Mr. and Mrs. Washington, dinner was great," I said while walking out of the front door,".

"No problem baby, come again," Kelsey's mother said while bringing me in for a hug.

"Yeah son it was nice meeting you, remember what we talked about," Her father said while squeezing my shoulder. I silently flinched.

"I will sir,"

"Mom and Dad I'm going to go with him to his car," Kelsey

said while grabbing my head. They both nodded and then she followed me out of the door.

"Baby they loved you!" She squealed while pulling me into a hug. I smiled and kissed her lips softly.

"I told you babe I'm going to get going now, I don't want hear my mother's mouth,"

Okay, call me as soon as you get in," She said while kissing my nose.

"I will babe I promise, now go back in before your father kills me," She smiled kissed me and then went back in. As soon as I closed the door to my car I sighed in relief that's one thing I can cross off of my list now I have to just keep my baby satisfied.

Young Love

Kelsey

"Chic Salon, how may I help you?" I asked when I answered the front desk phone.

My mother had held me hostage all morning at her salon and I hadn't sat down yet. I thanked God things were slowing down. The morning rush was ridiculous.

Hey my baby, what you doing today?

I smiled instantly. It was a text from Calvin. We've been dating for three months now and he's absolutely amazing.

Nothing much I'm at my mom's job super bored

Ask her if I can steal you for a min.

I looked down at the text and blushed instantly.

Only because I miss you

I walked towards my mother's station to ask her if I could take off for lunch. She and my dad met Calvin and they adored him so I'm sure it wouldn't be that much of an issue.

My dad was a little iffy at first, but he came around eventually.

"Mommy, can I go to lunch with Calvin?"

She adjusted the wide frame Raybans on her face and smiled at me through the mirror.

"Yeah, text me when you get there, do you need money?"

"No. I'm good thanks, love you."

'She said I can come.' I quickly texted him.

'Cool I'm already here come out.' I grabbed my purse and walked towards the entrance.

"Bye everyone!" I yelled over my shoulder.

I looked at Calvin as he stood in front of his car with his hands in his pockets waiting for me.

"Look at you looking so good." he joked while pulling me by my waist. "Who you looking all good for?" he whispered into my ear.

"For my boyfriend."

He let out a light laugh. "Keep playing with me Kelsey and you're going to get more than you asking for."

I looked up at him and laughed. "You are so nasty!" I playfully hit his chest.

"I know but I have a right to be when it comes down to my girl, give me the luscious."

I reached up and pecked his lips.

"What do you want for lunch?" I asked.

"I don't know; it's up to you," he said while looking at his phone.

"Ooh babe; let's go that Jamaican juice bar!"

Calvin lightly laughed. "Damn Ma, don't get too excited."

I smiled. "I can't help it, that Jerk chicken was so good." I moaned and he shook his head.

"Before I forget, stand here." He jogged to the back of his car.

I stood there waiting for him, wondering what he was doing. A few seconds later, he came back with two big Bloomingdales bags.

"Here, since you love these shits so much."

I looked in the bags and back up at Calvin. I bit my bottom lip and then reached up to kiss his lips.

"Why are you so good to me?" I asked.

"This is my job and to see you smile is my paycheck, you like 'em?" He asked.

He was referring to the two pairs of Uggs that were in the bags.

"I love them, thank you." I kissed him once more.

"That's all that matters, let's go eat now."

For Calvin to only be 17, he possessed qualities of a man. His constant worry for me and my happiness makes me view things differently.

Some grown men moan and groan about buying things for their wives, I've seen it. Calvin acted as if it was nothing, like it was the simplest thing.

If being single for that long is what it took for me to find Calvin, I'd wait and be lonely even longer. Many call it puppy love, but no matter what it is, it's good enough for Calvin and I and that's all that really matters.

You Go Boy

Calvin

"What's up Mommy?" I walked up behind my mother and kissed her cheek lightly.

"Good morning baby boy, excited?" She asked.

Today was the day I'd been looking forward to all season. I heard a scout from UCLA was going to be at the game and that was all that had been going through my mind. I had to figure out how I could catch his attention and show him my skill.

"Yeah, are you coming to my last game today?" I reached for an apple and bit into it.

"Do I miss any others, Calvin?"

I smiled lightly. My parents and Kelsey supported me unconditionally. They hadn't missed any games since the season began.

"Nah not at all, what you in here cooking?" I was so close to lifting the lid when she slapped my hand.

"Nosey, what did I tell you about touching my pots? How's my girl though?" She asked while putting the top back to its original place.

"Who?" I knew she was talking about Kelsey; I was just

messing with her.

"Play with me boy; I'm talking about my daughter in law!" At times, I think my mother likes Kelsey more than I do.

"She's good, matter of fact; I need to text her and tell her I'm picking her up this morning so we can chill after the big game." I pulled my phone out and sent her a quick text.

"Alright do you; just make sure y'all not late and when are you cutting your hair?" She pulled at my short curls that had begun to grow out.

"I'm not, I'm just going to keep lining it up, plus Kelsey likes it."

"Well I don't, but I can't force you to get rid of it. Just make sure you keep it looking neat. I will not have my son walking around here looking like a booga wolf."

I laughed lightly. "Alright Ma, you just love to fuss." I kissed her forehead.

"I wouldn't be me if I didn't, now go before you and Kelsey are late."

I nodded and pulled out my phone to text Kelsey and tell her I was going to come pick her up.

'Good morning baby, I hope you slept well I also hope your ass is up and ready by the time I get there' I laughed lightly as I sent the text. I loved messing with her especially when it came down to time.

It was sweet up until you had to ruin it lol, but no need babe Aria and I are already here prepping the halls for the big game

Alright see you later then. I slid my phone back in my pocket grabbed my stuff and was out.

Kelsey

"Aria, we both can't reach!" We struggled to plaster the two signs on the bulletin board across from the main office.

"I know, let's get one of the boys to do it." She hopped off of the chair and scanned the hallway in search of Calvin and Dwayne.

To be honest, I was tired of doing this. We literally spent all day prepping the halls for the big game. The only reason I was doing this was because of community service hours.

"No, wait, I got it." I successfully hung the sign up. I looked down at my watch and checked the time.

"We've literally been here since 9 doing this." I stepped back and looked at the sign. It was still a bit crooked but it would do.

"I know, I know but before I forget, I have to spill the tea about Dwayne and Chris!"

"Wait, what happened?" I asked while picking up the stray papers that were scattered on the floor.

"Well, Dwayne and I were hanging out and Chris kept calling me. Dwayne snatched the phone, words were exchanged and then Dwa-"

I felt Calvin's long strong arms wrap around my thick waist, his crotch centered right on my butt.

His touch is so electrifying.

"Hey baby." I cooed while he nibbled on my neck gently.

"Wassup?" He pulled me away and spun me around. I watched as he eyed my leggings and I just knew he was going to complain.

"Why you wearing these though?" He pulled at my leggings.

I rolled my eyes and put my hands on my hip. "They looked cute with my outfit, especially my boots." I smiled, referring to the chestnut UGGS he bought for me not too long ago.

"Yeah, well only wear them when you're with me. I'd hate to have to kill somebody. I'm your man and I have to refrain myself from touching all on you, imagine a random dude in the street."

I rolled my eyes.

"Whatever, where are you and Dwayne headed to?" I asked, changing the subject.

"We came to pick y'all up for lunch." He pulled me close and wrapped his arms around my waist.

"Babe, we can't even come. We have to finish decorating the halls for your game."

"That's cool; you want me to get you something?" He asked.

"Yeah." I reached up to pick a small piece of lint off of his sweater.

"What you want?"

"Panera Bread."

He smiled. "Your ass is too spoiled." Calvin just loved saying that.

"How?" I stuck my bottom lip out.

"You talking about Panera Bread and that's mad far. I'm not going to complain though, I have gas. I'm going to call you when I get there so I won't forget what you want."

I smiled and kissed him lightly. I took my thumb and wiped my lip gloss off his lips.

"Let me go so I can be back in time." He pulled me closer.

"Alright, if we aren't in here, we are in Ms. Mitchell's room."

He nodded and walked towards Dwayne.

Damn he treats me so special.

From the corner of my eye I could see Imani staring. Her eyes were fixated on me and if I'm not mistaken, I could see tears at the brim of her eyes.

I shook my head and walked towards Aria, whose face was screwed up. Her hand was on her hip and she tapped her foot in an impatient way.

"Now, what happened?" I asked.

"Your done being all lovey- lovey over there?" She spoke sarcastically.

"Just shut up and tell me the tea."

Calvin

"Bro, I'm so close to smacking the dog shit out of Aria's ex!" Dwayne screamed as we pulled into Panera Bread's parking lot.

"What happened?" I asked.

"Yesterday night we chilling and having a good time. This bum called her like 60 times messing up the flow of the night, so you know I had to handle him. I called him back and then he tried to be on some wreck shit. He was talking about I know where he stay, so I told him what's up anytime anywhere. He got shook and hung up." He gripped the dashboard.

"Calm down, he's not worth it. You know he is a bum. Your head needs to be in this game today, and not on his bum ass."

"I know but I'm really close to breaking him up. You know how I am, bro."

"I know and I'm telling you to chill. He'll get his, don't worry. Just leave it alone for now and if he do it again, then you know wassup. I'm rocking with you." I opened my door, stepped out and he did the same.

"I'm chilling bro, for now."

"Yeah, just chill. Let him keep burying himself."

"You right, you right."

No one knows Dwayne like I do, that's like my brother so I know him pretty well. His temper is crazy. When he fights, he fights to kill. That's the last thing he needed to worry about, especially if he's trying to go to college. If calming him down was going to work, then that's what I have to do. All I know is this Chris dude better chill because he has no idea who he's messing with.

Support System

Kelsey

"Woooo Calvin!" I screamed. My baby was killing tonight. I must admit he was putting on.

"Yeah, baby boy!" I looked over at Calvin's little support system. The group consisted of both Dwayne and Aria's parents, along with my mother and father. We looked like the damn Brady Bunch; we each had on these pullover hoodies with Calvin and Dwayne's pictures plastered on the front.

The energy in the stands was crazy! As expected though, our school was up against Wilburn. That school was one of the best, alongside Chadrich of course, in football.

Calvin was so focused and in the game. He'd occasionally glance up in the stands and smirk and I'd blow him a kiss. His focus went right back to the game.

A couple of girls in the stands saw our plays of affection and weren't too happy. That made me even happier, I had something that they all aspired to have and there was nothing possible anyone could do about it.

It was halftime and my stomach was grumbling, I needed something to eat and quick! I stood and pulled my jeans up.

"Do you guys want anything from the snack bar?" I asked

while turning to face all of our parents.

"Just get us some waters, baby girl." My mother handed me a crispy twenty.

"I have it Mom."

I bumped Aria's shoulder to get her attention. "Come with me." I said.

"Fine." She stood up and walked with me to the indoor concession stand.

"Girl, I need to tell you something!" Aria leaned in and whispered.

"Why are you whispering?" I mocked her voice.

"What I'm about to say is confidential." She paused and looked around the large space to see if anyone could hear her.

"Well, say it, damn!"

"Dwayne well he umm… I let him umm…"

My eyes got wide.

"You guys had sex!?" I whispered harshly.

"No! He gave me oral sex." She mumbled.

"What, I can't understand you." I said trying to piece together whatever she was saying.

"God, Kelsey you can't hear." She reached up and whispered in my ear. If my eyes weren't wide then, they definitely were now. I pulled away from her.

"So y'all like." I tilted my head to the side.

"Yeah we." She mirrored my movement.

"Well, how was it?" I asked, sounding like a curious 12 year old.

"To be honest, it was amazing, like it just happened." She gawked while looking off into space.

I started to think about Calvin and I. Even though Calvin had playfully hinted at sex, we hadn't taken it serious and the issue hasn't affected our relationship before. If it began to, we'd cross that bridge when we get there.

"So why is Imani looking over here?" Aria grabbed my arm to look in her direction.

"She's been doing that for a minute now, it's irking me."

"So let's go ask her what the problem is!" Aria walked started towards Imani but I pulled her back quickly. Aria was the type to slap first and ask later.

"No, this is Calvin and Dwayne's day. I'm going to handle it, just not right now. This isn't the time or place." I spoke truthfully. Our parents were here and that was embarrassment neither of them needed.

"Alright, let's go before my hand starts to twitch." Aria said.

I shook my head and laughed.

"Come on." I grabbed her hand and we walked back towards the field.

The game had resumed and Wilbur was leading by one point. There was 10 seconds left on the clock and my baby was running to the end zone.

He was running through the group of buys that tried to surround him and it was like his feet were nonexistent. He successfully made it to the end zone and the crowd went crazy. I jumped up and ran towards him, his arms held me up as my legs wrapped around his waist.

"I'm so proud of you baby," I kissed all over his face. He was sweaty, but so what. I was proud. He laughed and put me down.

"Thank you babe." the crowd started to disperse and we walked towards where everyone else was.

"Look at my groupie section!" Calvin yelled.

We all sucked our teeth.

"I'm just playing, I appreciate it y'all." I stood beside him with my arm thrown around his shoulder and his arm stayed tightly around my thick waist.

"Yo' Cal', that was a good game." someone who was exiting the football field complimented.

"Thanks bro!"

"Ma, where's Pops?" He asked his mother, Kim.

"He had to leave a little early, he had a meeting." She answered in a low tone of voice.

"He couldn't stay a little while longer?" Calvin asked.

"I'm sorry ba-"

"Ma, no need to explain. I should've knew he couldn't stay for long." He turned to face me. His face was full of disappointment.

Calvin had told me prior to the game how busy his father was and how much it would interfere with their relationship, even though their bond was so close. Their relationship reminded me so much of my Dad and I, We were close but distant all at the same time. Both of our parents have strenuous work schedules that can put a strain on our relationships, and sometimes they don't understand have stressful that is.

72

"Here, go to my car. I'm going to go shower and change." He handed me the keys to his car and walked towards the small tunnel that led to the locker room.

Kim, Calvin's mother turned her head and watched him walk away, I knew she felt just as upset to see how hurt Calvin was. She finally spoke after gathering her thoughts.

"What are you guys doing after?" She said while turning her attention back to me.

"Nothing special, probably go to a diner." I answered.

"Alright, please be safe." She moved a bit closer to me and whispered in my ear.

"Talk to him for me, please." She kissed my cheek and walked away.

"Call me when you get home, Dwayne!"

"Aria, you too, do not be late." Both Aria and Dwayne's parents yelled while exiting the school. Aria and I walked to Calvin's car.

"What's wrong with Calvin?" Aria asked.

"I don't know, but I'm going to ask him as soon as he comes out." I said while unlocking his car.

Aria got in the back while I waited on the outside for Calvin. I needed to know if my baby was okay or not because regardless of the situation, he checked on me constantly.

A few minutes later Calvin and Dwayne came walking out of the school. My baby was fine in anything he wore, even in a simple sweatsuit. A fresh pair of Nike Huaraches graced his feet, and the short curls he decided to recently start sporting, looked so perfect along with his fresh line up.

"Hey." I reached up and pecked his lips lightly.

"Wassup, you hungry because I'm ready to go ea-" he started but I didn't let him finish.

"Calvin, stop and talk to me. Tell me how you feel."

He hesitated for a minute and then finally spoke. "Man, he does this shit to me every game, it's always something." He sighed and ran his hand over his face.

"I know babe and I'm pretty sure he wanted to stay, but sometimes business interferes and trust I've gone through the same thing with my dad. It's just something we have to accept, no matter if we want to or not."

"I know, I just feel like sometimes he doesn't understand. This was the biggest game, a possible life changer and he couldn't stay long enough to say son I'm proud of you."

"Calvin you know your father is proud of you, there's no need to wonder about that."

"I know that but I wanted to hear it from his mouth." He lay back on the car and I stood in front of him.

"I can't tell you to not feel how you do, but I can tell you to talk to your father about how your feeling. I think it would help."

"Yeah, I guess."

"Don't be like that, Calvin. I really do think you should talk to him about it."

"I'm going to try."

"That's all you have to do." I reached up and pecked his lips again.

His lips curved into a smile. I watched as his hands reached out in front of me. He grabbed the loops of my jeans and pulled me close to him.

"Why are you so perfect?" He whispered in the crook of my neck.

I practically shivered under his touch.

"I'm not perfect babe, trust me." He smiled against my skin sending goosebumps all around.

"But you are to me, give me a kiss." He puckered his lips.

I kissed him sweetly and gently, that's how all of our kisses were. They were intimate and passionate and it made me long for more.

Calvin's strong hands traveled to my backside and gave it a light squeeze.

"What you been doing lately?" He looked behind me and then back up at me.

"What do you mean?" I asked while laughing lightly.

"Your just so thick, man I'm lucky." I pushed him away from me playfully and walked back towards the car.

"Where you going?" he asked.

"To the car because you need to gather your thoughts." I laughed and shook my head.

"That's how you're going to do me." He asked while laughing.

"Yep, plus I'm hungry." I climbed in and he followed suit.

"So am I." He looked down at my thighs and licked his lips.

"Boy bye, drive please." He laughed and started the car up.

I know I couldn't guarantee my advice would help, but at least I tried.

Comfortable

Calvin

"You don't care how you get on FaceTime with me, do you?" I asked Kelsey.

"Nope, you should appreciate me even when I look the worst." She smiled lightly. "I do baby, but a head scarf?" I laughed, but in all actuality I love how comfortable she was with me.

"So you want me to hang up? Because I'm surely not taking my scarf off."

"Who you getting an attitude with?" I asked her.

She rolled her eyes and ignored me so I decided to mess with her.

"Baby," I whined.

"What Calvin?" I scrunched my face up.

"Why you treating me like a stepchild?"

"You're being annoying, that's why."

"Oh word, I'm hanging up."

"No! No! I'm just playing baby."

"Oh alright." She smiled.

"Anyway, what you wearing?" I asked.

"Clothes." She grinned

"You got a smart ass mouth, you know that?"

"I've been told." she looked up and smirked.

"What you wearing though, tell me?" Truth be told, I wanted to know something. Sex is something I'd never pressure her into, but I did need something to hold me over.

"If you insist on knowing, I'm wearing your t-shirt." I smiled.

"That's it, are you wearing panties?"

"Uh-huh."

"What color?"

"Pink and blue lace." She bit her bottom lip. And I licked mine.

"Let me see." She shifted a bit and switched the camera. I waited anticipating those beautiful thick brown thighs, the ones I dreamed of at night, the ones I so desperately wanted to be between. So you could understand the disappointment when her ass thought it was funny to show me her middle finger. She was laughing hysterically.

"Your ass is so disrespectful. You will be driving yourself tomorrow."

Her laughing died down but her smile stayed and I couldn't help but do the same.

"Stop being so sensitive. Baby, I'm tired so I'm about to hit the sheets." She yawned.

"Well, give me a kiss before you go." She puckered her lips and playfully kissed the camera.

"Babe, before you go to bed go and find some cocoa butter. Your lips are dry." She straight faced me and then laughed.

"I can't stand you, goodnight." We both laughed, ending the

conversation two hours later.

I can't get enough of her.

Big Mistake

Kelsey

"Can I use the restroom?" I asked as politely as I could.

"Yes, take the pass."

I nodded and rushed out the classroom. I'd literally been holding my pee forever.

As I walked through the empty halls all that could be heard was the heel of my riding boots hitting the freshly waxed linoleum.

I turned the knob to the bathroom only for it to be locked. I sighed and walked towards the staircase to go to the 2nd floor, hoping that that floor's bathroom was open. The strong stench of weed hit me as soon as I opened the stairway door and I rolled my eyes.

One thing I hate most is when the dumbasses cut class, sit in the staircase all day and block you from getting where you need to go.

A group of people crowded the stairs, one of them being Tate and the other being Imani. Visibly, she was high.

I shook my head not at the fact that she was faded but because it was only two other girls and about ten other guys.

"Excuse me." I spoke loud and clear. They all turned and looked my way.

"Wassup Ma, you can't speak?" I heard Tate say.

"Hi." I kept walking until he blocked my way of going up the stairs.

"You need to go, like move." I slightly pushed him out of my way.

"Why you acting like that?" He asked.

I scrunched my face up in confusion. Not once have we ever had any serious conversation, so why would I say hello?

"Can you move?" I asked again, growing annoyed.

"Come on; just let me get a hug." His arms wrapped around my waist and gripped my butt roughly. Without hesitation, my hand connected with his face.

"This fat bitch just hit me." He grabbed the side of his face and released me out of his grip.

I pushed him and tried to walk out of the staircase but he caught the tail end of my hair and yanked me back.

I'm not sure what he was on but it must have been something strong if he thought it was okay to put his hands on me.

"Get the hell off of me." I pushed him once more.

"No bitch, you like to hit so I'm going to teach you a lesson." He tried to shove his tongue down my throat. Before our lips came in contact, I clawed at his face.

"Bitch!" He looked at me with the most grimacing eyes. His eyes were red and low. He held one of the most grimacing smirks ever. It was enough to intimidate you for forever. My back was up against the wall as I struggled to get loose from his tight grip. I could feel his hands fumble with the zipper on my jeans.

"What is wrong with you, why are you doing this?" I asked while pushing him off of me.

"You were supposed to be mine! I waited forever just to get a chance to talk to you and then I find out you with this pretty boy." He put his lips on my neck.

I cringed at the feeling.

"I bet he doesn't make you feel like this." He tried sliding his hands in my pants.

I struggled to push him off of me.

"Get off of me!" I took my knee and aimed it right in his groin.

"Shit!" he screamed. He bent down and held his crotch area tightly. I used that time to rush out of the now empty staircase. Its funny how not one of the other thirteen people in the staircase bothered to help me. They all just scrambled like a bunch of roaches.

As soon as I was out of there I rushed into the bathroom. I pushed the stall door open bent over and emptied all of the contents of my stomach out in the toilet. I was literally sick to my stomach, I was beyond disgusted.

I felt so violated like a piece of trash. I reached into my back pocket and grabbed my cellphone.

My fingers tapped against the screen rapidly as my chest heaved up and down. I was in complete and utter shock and the only person I could talk to right now at this moment was Aria.

'Can you please meet me on the 2nd floor I'm in the bathroom.'

In a matter of minutes I could hear the bathroom door open.

Aria came walking towards me with a look of confusion so evident on her face.

"What's wrong, did your period come on, you need a pad?"

I shook my head. "No it's something else, it just happened." I fumbled over my words a bit.

She looked down at my hand that was trembling violently and then back up at my face. I parted my lips to speak but the words seemed to never leave my lips. All I could do was cry. The tears that had been stinging the back of my eyes for what felt like forever finally began to shed. Aria rushed over towards me and wrapped her arms around my body.

"What happened?"

I stopped for a bit trying to gather the thoughts that were racing.

"Kelsey, tell me!" She yelled.

"I-I…" the words began to spill right out of my mouth as if they'd been waiting to tell someone what happened.

"He did what!" she screamed.

"Aria, it happened so fast." I said through sniffles. I looked up at Aria's toffee colored skin and I could tell she was beyond pissed. Her face was a bright red and she gnawed at her bottom lip roughly.

"I'm going to kill him." She hopped off of the marble covered sink and started to walk towards the bathroom's exit. I grabbed her before she could go anywhere.

"If he put his hands on me, what do you think he's going to do to you?"

"I don't care Kelsey. He can't put his hands on you and think that there is no consequences."

"I don't want you getting involved Aria, please."

"Fine. I'm just going to tell your dad." She reached for my phone and I quickly grabbed it back.

"No Aria, you know how my father is."

She looked at me and then sighed. "You know what Kelsey you need to tell someone. If not your father, then tell Calvin."

My heart dropped to the pit of my stomach. Calvin hadn't crossed my mind at all. I knew that Calvin wouldn't take this well but I also knew he wouldn't take it as bad as my father would. My father's temperament when it came to me, his babygirl, was short to none. If he had to kill someone, he would. If he had to get my uncles involved, he would and that's something I'm convinced Tate wasn't ready for.

"I will, I promise."

She looked at me and then pulled me into a tight hug. "I'm sorry you had to go through that, Kelsey. Honestly you didn't deserve that."

I could feel the tears escape my eyes once again. "Thank you Ari."

She held me tighter. "You're my sister; you know I have your back."

The bell rang signaling that the transition of classes were about to begin. Luckily I had lunch so I could cool myself down.

"Let's go, okay." Aria pulled me out of the bathroom and into the crowded hallway. I looked down at the hall pass that I had forgotten to give back in.

"What about this?" I held the laminated paper that read Mrs. C's hall pass up for Aria to see.

She fanned her hand. "Girl, she'll get over it. Right now you just relax."

I nodded and placed the pass on top of my locker. I looked at myself in the small pink mirror that hung on the inside of my locker. My eyes were red and puffy from the crying and my skin had begun to dry up.

I grabbed my pocket size Shea moisture lotion and rubbed it into my dark brown skin, giving it a nice bronze shine. I grabbed my bag that Aria had gotten from the classroom for me and threw it on my shoulder. I pulled my hair into a neat ponytail and closed my locker.

I could feel strong hands cover my dark brown eyes and I instantly knew it was Calvin. I covered his hands with mines and rubbed them softly.

"Hi beautiful." He removed his hands, reached down and kissed my cheek. I turned to face him and smiled lightly.

"Hi baby." My voice came out a bit more somberly than expected.

"What's wrong?" He asked.

"What do you mean?" I looked away from him. He pulled my chin towards him and spoke sternly.

"You know what I mean, baby you don't look like yourself."

I looked away trying to gather my thoughts. I'm not sure if I wanted to let him know what happened just yet, but it looked like I had no choice. I felt he could read me like a book and catch on to my feelings.

"Calvin, I need to tell you something."

"What's up?" I turned away and then looked back at him. He grabbed my hand and brought his lips to the front of my hand.

"Tell me."

"Earlier today Tate he, he um." It was almost like I couldn't get the words out. It was like it was stuck in my throat. I watched as he clenched his jaws tightly.

"He what?"

"He groped me and then he pu-" Before I could say anything, he cut me off.

"Say no more." He dropped his bag to the floor and then slightly picked up his pants. He started to walk towards someone. For some reason, I already knew who he had seen.

I turned to face where he was looking and there Tate was, walking out of the school's bathroom. I grabbed Calvin's arm before he could go any further because I knew he was about to do some serious damage.

"Baby, please just relax." The last thing I needed was for him to go and beat Tate up. That would just kick up my anxiety even more.

"Let me go Kelsey." He said sternly.

"Calvin please, I don't want you to get in any trouble. He's not worth it."

"Was he worrying about getting into trouble when he touched my girl? No! So I'm not worried about trouble." He started to walk away from me but I grabbed him.

"Babe please, he isn't worth it."

"No but you are, he's not about to disrespect my girl and think it's cool." He snatched away from me and stormed towards Tate.

I rushed behind him, trying to keep up the pace.

"Calvin!" I yelled but he ignored me. As he neared Tate, his hands balled into a fist.

"Yo, so you pussy now?" Calvin asked Tate.

"Wh-" Before Tate could finish, Calvin's fist connected with Tate's face and he pummeled him with punches, giving him no mercy.

"Calvin!" I screamed.

"I should kill your ass, do you hear me?" Calvin said while throwing punches all around Tate's body. Dwayne rushed over and tried to pull Calvin off of Tate, but it was no use. I never saw this side of Calvin and quite frankly, it scared me.

Calvin picked Tate up by his collar and slammed him against the wall.

"Yo Calvin I'm sorry, please stop." Tate pleaded.

"Stop Calvin!" I screamed, but he didn't budge. His grip on Tate's collar got tighter.

I tried pulling him off, but I couldn't. Calvin was way too strong.

"Baby stop! He's not worth it!" I yelled again.

"The next time I hear you messed with my girl in any way, I'm killing your ass fuck boy, do you hear me!?" Tate nodded and Calvin brushed through the crowd, leaving Tate to squirm around on the floor.

I walked behind him and went with him to his car. He roughly opened the door.

"Get in." He pointed to the seat and I slid in. As soon as he got in, I couldn't help but feel angry and bad all at the same time. I feel like I was the cause of the commotion but I also feel angry at Calvin for letting Tate get to him. He has so much going for him and that all could've been taken away from him just by his actions today.

"Are you out of your mind Calvin? You jeopardized everything you've been working for today!" I yelled.

He gripped the steering wheel to the point where his knuckles were turned a pale white color.

"You have to understand how disrespectful that is, not only to you, but to me too! He put his hands on you baby!" He hit the dashboard, causing me to jump. He sighed and ran his hand over his face.

"I'm sorry I really am, but baby he had to face his consequence. With every action it's just that, a consequence follows behind."

I sighed and looked down his knuckles. They were beginning to swell. I reached in the backseat and grabbed his gym bag. I knew he carried a first aid kit, due to the season, so that's just what I was searching for. I pulled out a few alcohol pads and began to clean the small cuts that covered his swollen knuckles.

"Sss." He hissed.

"Baby you have to understand my job is to protect you and make sure you never have to worry. I wasn't there to do that today, I couldn't protect you. But after seeing what I did to that punk ass bitch today, no dudes are going to mess with you because they know I don't play that. They know what's up."

I delicately cleaned the remainder of the cuts.

"Baby I appreciate it, but I want you to think about it next time. Like you said there's a consequence for every action, you could've gotten in some real trouble today." I said while wrapping the ace bandage around his hand.

"I understand that babe, I do." He leaned forward and pecked my lips two times.

"But you have to understand, I have a job and that's to make sure you're good." I grabbed his ears and kissed him softly.

"You are doing your job and you're doing it perfectly." He bent down to kiss me but before he could, a light tap on the window stopped him. It was Dwayne and Aria. Calvin blew out a breath and rolled the window down.

"Damn man, you fucked him up." Dwayne said loudly.

Aria slapped him in the back of his head.

"Damn bae, what was that for?" He asked.

"For being loud. Anyway, how are you feeling Kelsey?"

"I'm okay, just ready to go home. This day was too much for me."

"I can understand; you want me to come with you?" I looked at Calvin and then back at her.

"No boo, I'm okay." She nodded and walked off with Dwayne.

Even though today was a lot to deal with, I can honestly say this had brought Calvin and I even closer. What I feel for him is a feeling I've never had before. I can only hope he feels the same for me.

Good Vibes

Kelsey

I ran my fingers through my hair in awe. My mother had agreed to silk press Aria and I's hair for a little party that we were going to tonight.

"I'm feeling myself, I'm feeling myself!" Aria sung off key from the bathroom.

I rolled my eyes and knocked on the door loudly.

"Can you hurry up!? No one asked for a concert!"

A few minutes later, Aria popped out of the bathroom.

"You know what, you're so rude!" I smiled lightly.

"Whatever, what time are we leaving?" I asked while applying some mascara to my eye lashes.

"10, 10:30." I nodded and looked at my phone.

"We need to leave soon then, it's already 9:45." I leaned over and laced up my sneakers.

I decided to keep it simple tonight. I picked out a pair of dark denim jeans, a loose fitting black t-shirt, and a pair of black Miu-Miu sneakers.

I walked inside my closet and pushed a few hangers around, contemplating on which jacket I should wear.

"Ari, black motorcycle jacket or red one?" I screamed from my closet.

"Red moto." She yelled back.

I nodded and slid it on my arms. I reached up and grabbed my red leather Rebecca Mink off bag to match. I walked towards the full body mirror and turned to see my side profile. I smiled in approval. I walked out to see Aria dressed, which was surprising. She's normally the last to get ready.

"See I'm ready." she boasted.

"Whatever, it only took me yelling at you!" I took my phone off of its charger.

"We look good!" she screamed.

"I know and love that dark lip." I complimented her dark chocolate lipstick color. It contrasted with her complexion perfectly. She smiled and walked out the door.

"Thank you, compliments of Dwayne's credit card."

I shook my head.

We walked downstairs and towards my parents, who were cuddled up on the couch.

"Mommy, we are about to leave."

She looked at the time.

"At 10:30? What time are y'all coming home?" She asked.

"2." I muttered.

"2, you must be smoking, little girl? Y'all better be home by 12."

"Come on Mom that's not right, a party doesn't start until like 12. Come on." I whined.

"No." She said quickly.

I sucked my teeth.

"Mommy I never go out, come on just this one time." I stuck my bottom lip out.

"So because you never go out I'm supposed to disregard my rules."

I turned to my dad.

"Daddy, help me out here."

"Come on babe, she's a good girl. We have to trust her." She rolled her eyes and then finally gave in.

"Fine, fine! But y'all behinds better be here at 2. Not 2:01 or 2:03, but 2 on the dot."

We shook our heads in confirmation.

"One more request."

My mother gave me a pointed look.

"You're pushing it little girl, what is it?"

"May I please take the Porsche?" I asked.

"Yes you may."

I smiled and grabbed the keys off of the counter. We started walking towards the front door but she stopped us.

"Wait a minute now, I didn't say y'all could walk away yet."

I sighed a little and walked back towards her.

"No drinking, that's the first rule. If you put your cups down and walk away from them, that's it. Leave it there, it's no good, and be ladies at all times."

We nodded in confirmation.

"Thank you Mama I love you so much!" We both kissed her cheek lightly.

"Uh-huh. Spoiled ass. Go on, time is ticking away."

"Thanks Daddy." I kissed his cheek lightly too.

"I got y'all babygirls, have fun!"

We walked in and I must admit the scene was dope, but from what Aria said Bradford's parties are always hot. I've never been to a party so I don't really have much to compare it to. Bradford's home was set up like an upscale nightclub and it was packed just like one half of Jersey was in here.

"Let me take your coat boo." Aria yelled over the music. I handed it to her and started to scan the crowd.

Calvin said he was here already so that's who I was looking for. The crowd was thick and I found myself jumping up and down searching for him that was until I spotted him. And when I tell you he looked good, I meant it.

The Five panel Supreme snapback he wore hung low over his eyes and a red solo cup occupied his hand. I walked up behind and tapped his shoulder lightly. He turned around and surveyed my body.

"Hi baby." I said low. He looked at me for a while and sunk his teeth in his bottom lip. It took him a while to speak and when he finally did it sent me over edge.

"Damn baby, you look good." His voice was deep and raspy and I found that so attractive.

I could say the same. He looked so fresh and clean. The black long sleeve tee he wore was so crisp and neat. The burgundy material in his hat matched his Balenciaga's almost perfectly.

Fine wasn't even the word.

"You too baby." I bit my lip as I watched him lick his bottom lip.

"Why are you looking at me like that?" I asked.

"I can't stare at my baby?" He pulled me to him by my waist.

"You can stare all you want baby, even if it's a little weird."
He laughed lightly.

"Why are you trying to call me a low key creep?"
I giggled lightly.

"I'm not, I'm just saying."

I looked at the brown liquid in his cup and reached for it. "Let me taste it."

He scrunched his face up.

"You not ready for this Ma"

I rolled my eyes and pursed my lips together.

"How do you know what I'm ready for? Let me taste it."

He gave me his cup and let me take a small sip. I scrunched my face up and slapped my hand on my chest. "That's disgusting, how could you drink that?" I asked.

He laughed. "I told you that you weren't ready for this but just had to try it."

I playfully mushed his forehead.

"Whatever."

He pulled me close to him.

"You're so fine, you know that?" I could feel myself blushing already.

"I've been told." I said smartly.

"Look at you being all cute and shit." His hands rubbed my butt softly.

"You think I'm cute? Yes or No? Yes?" I laughed lightly

mocking an Instagram video that had gone viral.

"You're so childish man I swear." Calvin said.

I smiled.

"Give me a kiss." I said.

He reached down and kissed me hungrily. My hands rubbed the back of his head as our tongues danced to each other's beat.

"Can y'all be nasty somewhere else, Lord!" I could hear Aria say sarcastically.

We pulled away. I reached up and wiped some of my gloss off of his lips.

"You always have something to say man." Calvin said jokingly.

"I'm just saying must you try to get her pregnant at this very moment!"

I looked at her and rolled my eyes.

"You need a filter for your mouth."

"Yeah, yeah whatever, here." She handed me a frozen Daiquiri. From the looks of it, was a strawberry one. I took a sip.

"This is good, baby want to try this?" I put the straw up to Calvin's lips.

He took a sip while his arms stayed planted around my waist.

"It's good right?" He nodded while gripping my waist tightly.

"Alright bye guys, I see my baby." She walked off towards Dwayne.

"Baby this party is so dope, I swear."

"It is man. Especially because you're here."

"Why are you being so damn sweet tonight?" It felt like he

was saying all of the right things.

"I'm just speaking the truth."

I blushed uncontrollably. "Can you like stop?" I looked down.

He picked my chin up with his fingers.

"Stop what?" He licked his lips seductively.

"That! You have this I want to jump on you right now face."

"Maybe I do." I smiled and shook my head.

This was going to be a long night. I just knew it.

Calvin

The sexual tension in the room between Kelsey and I was beyond thick. What can I say though? My baby was looking good tonight and I'm pretty sure she knew that.

"Damn." I said low as Kelsey's thick hips grinded into me. All night we'd been playing with each other and it was all fun and games up until Little Cal started acting up. I wrapped my arms around her stomach, bent down and whispered in her ear.

"You feel what you doing to me?" I asked as I pushed myself into her so she could really feel what affect her body was having on me.

Kelsey was the perfect package. She had a pretty face, she was smart, ambitious and in my eyes had a beautiful body to match her beautiful personality. If only everyone was as lucky as I was.

The lights were dim and the music was loud enough to block out any of what I was saying.

"I'm really trying, but all this ass up on me is really tempting me."

"Tempting you to what?" She asked.

I reached down and kissed her neck lightly knowing that was her most sensitive spot.

"Mmm. Stop." I licked the sensitive spot and then began to suck on her neck roughly.

"B-baby that's going to leave a mark." She said low. That's just what I wanted to do: I wanted everybody to see that I was marking my territory.

"So what?" I kept sucking on her neck until I felt it was enough and a purplish mark appeared.

"I hate you." She hit my chest.

"What I do?" I asked playing innocent as she wiped her neck.

"You know what you did."

"I can't remember, my bad." I smirked slyly and looked past her.

"Uh-huh." She rolled her eyes and took a sip of her frozen drink.

Drake's *Jungle* began to play throughout the party and the sexual tension that went away a minute ago, returned stronger than ever. She rocked her hips directly on me along to the beat.

I have to admit these last couple of months that we've been together she's been getting bolder and bolder. I see she's been letting me in more. I can't lie and say I'm not happy either, this is the happiest I've ever been and my baby is all to blame for that.

Despite the last incident that took place with me and that fuck boy Tate, she's been showing signs of being happy too. Let's hope it stays this way.

Patience

Calvin

"Calvin, can you hurry up? I'm hungry." Kelsey whined.

"Alright, it'll be quick. Here, take the key so you won't be in the cold." She grabbed the keys out of my hand and walked towards my car.

This was the second time I left my wallet and phone in my locker and I'm not sure how. I rushed through the hallway towards my locker. Kelsey wasn't in the best of moods today. She was grumpy and ready to eat so I knew I had to hurry and rush out.

"Hey Calvin." I looked over my shoulder and sighed. It was Imani, the infamous Imani. I just hit her with the head nod.

You know that one female you regret ever messing with? Yeah, that's her. After I had sex for the first time I started messing with every female, cute or ugly, just to say I did it. But as I grew up, I grew out of that. Unfortunately, Imani hadn't reached that stage yet. I blocked her from every social media website known to man.

She'll try to make you slip up like that and I wasn't having that at all. I saw how she was with my friends even after she knew they were in relationships. She had a couple screws loose, I won't lie. That's partially why I stopped messing with her.

"Why are you acting like that, you don't remember two

summers ago? I was good enough then."

I sighed and shook my head. I continued to ignore her. She wanted me to engage in a conversation with her and it wasn't going to happen. I'm good on all that. I could feel her walk up behind me.

"I'm not your precious little Kelsey; I bet she can't take it like I could. I know you miss me." She reached around and grabbed me through my pants. I pushed her away.

"Yo you nuts or something, your ass must've been smoking too much weed."

"Come on Calvin, one last time and I'll leave y'all to be as happy as y'all claim." She started to fidget with my belt buckle. All that was going through my mind was if my baby walks through that door I'm dead. In a split second, I pushed her up against the locker.

"The fuck is wrong with you, you can't hear! Are you bugged the fuck out!"

She flinched and turned her head.

"Baby I tol-" I looked over at Kelsey. She clutched onto her purse tightly with a look I couldn't stand to see. I let Imani go and walked towards her.

"Baby, it's not what you think, I prom-." She put her hand up to stop me. I can't lie and say I wasn't nervous as to what would happen next because I was.

Kelsey

I should've expected this from Imani. I didn't want to, though. I really did want to give her the benefit of the doubt that she wasn't going to make a move on Calvin, but I should've known.

Calvin's face was stone and full of shock as it should be. I wanted to know why she was in my boyfriend's face and why was he allowing it, but I refuse to let her see I and Calvin argue.

"Baby, I'll be right out. You can go warm your car up." I reached up and laid a sloppy wet kiss on his lips just to piss her off.

Deep down inside though I wanted to slap the piss out of Calvin for letting her be in his face.

"You… you sure?" Calvin asked, stuttering a bit.

"Yep." He nodded, grabbed his things along with mine and walked towards his car. I turned my attention back to Imani, whose face was now beet red.

"What's wrong with you?" I asked.

She hesitated for a minute and twisted her lips up as if she was thinking of what to say next.

"We had sex!" Imani blurted out.

"No you did not." I said plainly. I knew when someone was lying and this girl indeed was lying.

"If you don't believe me check your *man's* phone."

"You are so sad. My "man" wouldn't ever be associated with

you, he's said it himself. I don't know what you're aiming for or what you're aiming to do but it'll never work, you know why? Because my "man" shows great restraint, especially when it comes down to females like you. I'm losing my patience and you need to get over Calvin, he doesn't want you. Now you can try all the tricks you want but my patience is running thin. You're lucky I was raised to be a lady and that I see college in the near future because if I was as pathetic as you, I would've beaten you up and down this hallway." I flipped my hair and walked off. That felt so good.

Just like that I walked away from her. I was done talking to her. She's not worth my time. But there was one person I did need to talk to and that was Calvin. I know I felt this girl is lying, but I need confirmation. I need for Calvin to tell me out of his mouth. As soon as I got closer to his car, he started speaking.

"Whatever lies she told you in there, don't believe them."

"Why was she talking to you?" I asked.

"She popped up out of nowhere, I swear." He looked at me intently.

"So nothing happened?" I questioned him again.

"Nothing baby."

I searched his face to see if the truth was there and I felt it. I felt he was being completely honest.

"I trust you so I'm going to take your word for it. But I'm warning you that she's always up to no good. She'll make me hurt her. Stay away from her just like I stayed away from Tate. I need you to do the same with this crazy ass girl."

He nodded and grabbed my hand. "It's done. I'll stay away,

you got it babe."

I nodded and walked ahead of him.

I really do hate getting out of character, especially like that, but she's been asking for it. I just hope she takes me seriously. I really hope she does because nothing about that threat was empty. I'm no fighter but if you push me there then I'm liable to snap

Calm Before the Storm

Tate

I stared at the small spot on the wall for what seemed like hours. My mind was vacant and my being on my fourth blunt wasn't helping at all. I inhaled and exhaled taking in the sweet taste of the blunt. I'd been smoking non-stop for three days and I didn't plan on stopping.

I wanted to drown everything out, especially that ass whopping I took from Calvin's punk ass. I don't know if I was madder at him or that bitch Kelsey. I wanted her from the beginning and now she's with some corny ass dude. In my mind Kelsey was mine and that was final.

The knocking on the door forced me out of my thoughts. I took another pull and then got up. The knocking on the door got louder.

"Coming, damn." I ashed my blunt and went to open the door.

"Damn." I said low. Imani Brinkston stood in front of my door, barely dressed. I took in her short petite frame and her long black silky hair. I can't lie and say she wasn't fine because she definitely was, but she's no Kelsey.

"Are you going to let me in or...?" She trailed off.

I stepped to the side and let her in.

"What's up, why are you here?" I asked her. She and I messed around a few times, nothing too serious. It was always for fun.

"I wanted to talk to you about something." She walked ahead of me, switching her hips in the process. She sat on the couch adjacent from me.

"Come, sit." I walked over and took a seat on my grandmother's plush couch.

"How you been, since the fight and everything?" She asked.

"I'm cool, ready for revenge but I'm cool." I sat and reached for my blunt and lighter. I put it out earlier because I thought it was my Grandmother at the door, but since it isn't I'm not about to waste perfectly good weed.

"It's funny that you bring up revenge." She smirked and looked at me.

"What?" I asked.

"I can imagine after what happened you're pretty upset with Calvin."

I nodded.

"Yeah, why?"

"Well, I hate Kelsey."

"Why?" I asked.

"Let's just say she took something that was mine and I want my payback."

"Alright, what does that have to do with me?" I asked.

"Well." She grabbed my thigh and looked in my eyes. "You help me and I help you." She began to rub me from the outside of my jeans.

"What I have to do?"

She smiled.

"Just follow my lead, that's all you have to do." She climbed on top of me and grabbed the blunt from my hand. She took a pull and exhaled.

I didn't know what I was getting myself into but she was saying all the right things right now. I felt her small waist and groped her ass.

"I'm down."

She smiled.

"Good, now where's your bedroom?"

I smirked and led her up the stairs. I'm making a deal with the devil, I just know it.

Calvin

"Get on my back." I told Kelsey.

"Umm no." She ate a piece of her cotton candy.

Today we had a little date and I have to admit I was enjoying every moment of it. Being around her just puts me in a place I can't describe. I looked down at her and stopped walking.

"You were just saying your feet were on fire, now come on."

"Calvin, if you drop me." She warned.

"Calm down; I'm not going to drop you." She looked at me and handed me her cotton candy.

"Here."

I took it from her and squatted down a little, giving her space to slide on my back. I stood up and adjusted her, grabbing a hold of her thick thighs.

We stayed this like a while and I can't lie and say I wasn't comfortable because I was.

"You good baby?" I asked her.

"I'm fine babe." She answered sweetly.

I smiled as we walked along the boardwalk.

"Babe, put me down. I want to take pictures in the photo booth." I put her down and we walked towards the small photo booth in the middle of the boardwalk. We sat down and she threw her arms around my shoulders.

I turned to face her and took this moment to admire her beauty. Her full chunky cheeks and her full pink lips, her beautiful dark skin and her dark brown eyes that glistened in the sunlight. I'm not trying to believe it but I'm falling so deeply in love with her. I don't know how exactly to deal so I'm going to just let it flow. Sooner or later I'm going to have to tell her how I feel and I just know it's going to be hard man.

"Ready?" she asked me.

"Yeah I'm ready." I answered her. She pulled me close to her and kissed my lips while the timer on the photo booth went off. I couldn't shake off the fact that she's so perfect.

Let's Talk About It

Kelsey

I lay on Calvin's chest while he napped silently. He released a couple of light snores, but nothing over the top. I ran my thumb along his bottom lip then down to his chest. He moved a bit but stayed asleep. His grip on my waist got tighter,

"Calvin?" I said softly.

"Hmm?" He mumbled.

"Wake up." I shook him lightly.

"C'mon Kelsey." he spoke tiredly.

I smiled lightly at his annoyance. "Baby, I want to talk."

He didn't answer this time.

I sighed. I really wanted to talk about something that had been bothering me for a while now. I looked up at Calvin who was dead to the world sleep.

I reached behind me, grabbed a pillow and hit him with it.

"Damn Kelsey. What do you want?"

I rolled my eyes.

"You know what? Forget it." I swung my feet around the bed and prepared to get up. He hopped up with quickness.

"Alright, alright I'm sorry, what you want to talk about?"

I sat back down and crossed my legs Indian style. I hesitated for a while but then warned him.

"You better not laugh either." I spoke seriously.

"You better talk before I go back to sleep."

"Fine, does sex ever cross your mind?"

"Yeah, why'd you ask?" He sat up and looked towards me.

"I don't know, I should've never said anything."

He laughed lightly.

"C'mon babe, just tell me."

"As you know I'm a virgin, and Aria and I were talking about sex. Her and Dwayne have been intimate and I feel kind of pressed to d-"

I was cut off by Calvin's obnoxious laugh, I pushed his shoulder roughly.

"What's so funny?"

His laughing died down a bit but it was still obnoxious and I was embarrassed.

"I'm your boyfriend and you're talking to me all professional. I get it though, I'm irresistible and you want me." He wiggled his eyebrows.

I rolled my eyes and sighed loudly.

"Boy, take several seats."

He laughed lightly. "Nah let me stop playing."

"Please do." I answered seriously.

"To be honest, I've thought about being with you but I'm not about to rush you. I know you're not ready and I'm willing to wait."

I smiled, reached up and kissed him. He pulled me closer and kissed my lips sweetly.

"You're so perfect," I spoke sincerely.

"Nah, you made me this way. Now, can I go back to sleep? " he questioned.

"Nope, my mother is going to be home in 30 minutes and if she sees your behind in here, we're both dead."

"So you're kicking me out?" he smiled and stood up.

"Pretty much." I got up and wrapped my arms around his waist.

"I respect it." He looked down at me and smiled.

"You're so beautiful," Calvin said.

I smiled and kissed his lips sweetly. If no one made me feel beautiful, Calvin sure did.

"Thank you baby, I kind of want to spend more time with you today." I said honestly.

"What do you want to do?"

"I don't know." I walked into my closet

"Let's go to the movies and then go eat." He suggested.

"Yeah, I've been wanting to see *Selma* for a while now." I pushed my hangers back and forth in search for something to wear.

I grabbed my denim jumpsuit off one of the hangers and held it up to my body, then I grabbed my long dark blue cardigan.

"This will do; now shoes."

I bit my bottom lip gently. I walked towards my organized shoe area and decided on my navy blue Christian Louboutin sneakers. I grabbed my clothes and laid them on my bed.

"Yo bro, let's link up. I know you're coming to the City and our pops' are working together so we definitely should do something soon."

I watched as Calvin talked on the phone. His bottom grills and pearly whites were shining bright. With Drake's *How about now* beat playing in the background, I was in my feelings.

I pointed to tell him I was going to the bathroom. He nodded and resumed his phone call.

I turned on my shower and let the water heat up. It made me crave the feeling of the hot water on my skin. I hopped in the shower and let the hot water beam down my back. After washing up a couple more times, I stepped out and grabbed my towel off of the porcelain sink. Taking a seat in front of my mirror, I decided to get started with my hair first. I decided to leave it curly today.

A perm has never graced my head and I must admit as I got older it's gotten harder to maintain. Thank God for my mother because if not, I would've been looking crazy. I reached for some curling pudding and massaged it into my scalp, it felt so good.

I pulled my thick hair up into a bun and applied some mascara to my already thick eyelashes. I put on a coat of gloss on my lips. I quickly grabbed my outfit and got dressed. I must admit, I looked cute. I walked out the bathroom and watched as Calvin continued to talk on the phone. He looked up and smiled.

"Yo Jus', I'll give you a call later." He hung up and sat his phone on the small table across from my couch.

"My baby so fine." he said while looking me up and down.

I laughed and playfully blew him a kiss.

I could say the same for him. He was dressed in black jeans that were a bit baggy. He had a black Kenzo t-shirt, his army green bomber jacket and black Timberland construction boots. Can he get any finer?

"You ready?" I asked while grabbing my phone.

"Yeah let's go."

"You know you need a Ryder bae." I sung to my camera. I put the camera on Calvin but he was too focused on driving to notice.

"Baby look!" I semi yelled over the music.

He looked over at me and smiled. "I just want you to need me." He sung off key.

I laughed and ended the video. I decided to put it on Instagram.

@_Princess. K I just want to be your Ryder. @Calvin powers_

I grabbed Calvin's hand as we walked inside the crowded theater.

"I'm going to the bathroom, I'll be back. Wait on line." Calvin instructed me.

I looked ahead at the concession stand line that damn near wrapped around the theater.

"Okay, what do you want?" I asked him.

"I'll probably get here before you get to the counter."

I nodded and walked towards the line, I felt my phone vibrate. I reached in my back pocket. There were a bunch of comments under Calvin and I's video. I decided to read a couple.

@Jolieeee Y'all so cute #goals

@Prettygirljamie Yasss I love you guys so much! Such a beautiful couple.

@Ariax_ He a lucky dude 'cause your mean ass like him.

I laughed and smiled to myself as I continued to scroll through the countless comments.

"Next!" the girl at the concession stand yelled with an attitude. I walked towards her and boy was it a sight to see.

Her purple weave was thin and in need of CPR, and her eyebrows were harshly penciled in.

"What can I get you today?" she asked. Her face was full of attitude. I decided to take my sweet time.

She rolled her eyes annoyed at my actions. I just made her wait a little longer.

"I'll hav-" I felt arms wrap around my waist.

"So you were about to let your man go hungry?" Calvin whispered in my ear.

Perfect timing, I thought to myself.

"Never that baby, what do you want?" I said while looking at the cashier. Today was a day where I felt like being petty.

"Whatever you get is fine."

I smiled and began to order.

"Umm. Let me get a large popcorn, two large Sprites, Skittles and Goobers."

She sighed lightly and walked off to get the stuff.

"Yo, what's her problem?" Calvin asked.

I shrugged my shoulders. "I don't know, she's been like that since she saw me."

"Jealousy at its finest, babe. If I was a girl I'd get mad when I look at you too." He kissed the tip of my nose and pulled out his phone.

I smiled to myself. It was things like this that make me feel so special.

The rude cashier came back and sat our food and drinks on the counter roughly. I smiled and shook my head.

"That'll be $20."

Calvin slid his card across the counter before I could reach for my wallet.

"Baby, I have it." I said to him.

He gave me a pointed look.

"I know you have it, but I'm paying." Calvin said sternly.

I sucked my teeth and rolled my eyes.

"Babe, come on. Stop acting like that please." Calvin leaned in and kissed the tip of my ear. I nodded my head as he continued to whisper in my ear.

"Hello, excuse me, somebody needs to pay!" The cashier said with an attitude.

I opened my mouth to speak but Calvin beat me to the punch.

"I don't know what your issue is but you need to calm down, especially when you're talking to my girl." The girl's cheeks turned red from embarrassment. She just took Calvin's credit card and swiped it. She punched in a couple of keys on the register and then handed the card back to him.

Calvin snatched the things of off the counter and then grabbed my hand.

"Rude ass people, man." He muttered under his breath as we walked off.

I turned to face the cashier and said. "Thank you and have a great day." I knew my voice was dripping sarcasm, and quite frankly, I didn't care. She deserved my attitude.

I looked at Calvin, who had the most annoyed expression on his face. I reached up and grabbed his face lightly.

"Babe, relax."

He looked at me and began to speak. "I'm good, just annoyed." He put his phone back in his pocket.

"Why?" I asked.

"I'm just tired of people, man." He sighed.

"Babe, don't let that girl get to you."

He looked at me and kissed my forehead. "I won't babe let's just enjoy our day."

I nodded. For some odd reason I felt the cashier wasn't the only thing bothering him. I shook it off and followed behind him into the small theatre. I'm sure if he was feeling annoyed about something he'd tell me.

It's apparent that I'm falling for Calvin, but I'm not quite sure how I feel about it.

Old News

Calvin

Regret slowly began to inch into me. After I dropped Kelsey off from our date, I had to handle some business. I was getting these text messages from Imani and I needed to handle her before she did or said anything to Kelsey. I sat in this greasy diner waiting for her to arrive. This is the last thing I wanted to do but I finally got Kelsey to open up to me and I'll be damned if I let anyone come in and ruin Kelsey and I's bond.

"I knew you missed me."

I shook my head.

"Nah, that's not what I called you for, sit down." She smiled lightly and slid into the small booth.

"What's up?" She said while licking her lips at me. I put my hand on the table and she tried to cover it. I snatched it back with quickness.

"This isn't that type of party, what are you texting my phone for?" I asked, getting straight to the point.

She sat back and smirked lightly.

"I miss you Calvin, honestly." I looked at her and scrunched my face up.

"What are you talking about?" I asked with confusion all over my face.

She leaned forward.

"I miss you, you don't miss me?" She asked.

"What is there to miss honestly? We messed around a few times in your mom's car." I said honestly. I was young, immature and ready to have sex with anything that wanted me. No matter the time or place, I was always game.

"That's how you really feel Calvin?" She said while leaning back in the small booth.

"Yes, so stop texting me. I don't want to upset my girl." I spoke truthfully. The last thing Kelsey needs to see is Imani texting my phone.

"Your girl? I wonder how your girl would feel about these." She reached in her purse and slapped some sonograms on the table.

"What the fuck is this?" I asked.

"You know exactly what these are." She smirked and looked at me with a satisfied grin on her face like she'd accomplished something.

"Yeah I know what they are, but why are you showing them to me?" I asked.

"Calvin, don't play dumb please?"

I started to really believe this girl was bugged out.

"I really don't have time for these bullshit ass games, what the fuck is wrong with you? Why are you showing me this?"

"Remember the last time we had sex, oh yeah unprotected sex that is, well I found out I was expecting. Of course you were the father to be but because I didn't want to make you feel uncomfortable, I aborted the baby. I did it for you Calvin." She grinned and reached for my hand, and yet again, I snatched it back.

"Yo you're sick, this conversation is over." I got up to leave but what she said next made me stop dead in my tracks.

"If you don't leave her, I'll make her leave you by leaking all of this stuff, including other pictures I have." Before I knew it, I had her small wrist in my hand.

"Don't play with me, I swear to God."

I could see her about to cry so I let her go. I don't believe in putting my hands on a female at all but she was pushing me there, so the best thing for me to do was leave.

I slammed the door to my car and sunk down in the seat. I thought back to all the times me and Imani messed around and I was starting to regret every single time I did anything with her.

I glanced down at my phone and a picture of Kelsey was my lock screen. Her beautiful dark skin glowed as she did a silly face. All I could think about was that face filled with tears if she ever found out what I and Imani did. I gripped my steering wheel tightly. When old news comes back around, you already know it's going to be destructive.

Celebration

Kelsey

"Mama Love, look at these." I pointed to the nude YSL heels that sat on Neiman Marcus's shoe rack. They were perfect and I needed them.

We were currently in Neiman's shopping for shoes. Calvin was invited to a huge New Year's Eve bash in the city and he, of course, was taking me as his date. I was excited and anxious all at the same time. Calvin told me how much he bragged about me to his friends and I was nervous as to how they'd take me.

The shoes were simple, yet glamorous, at the same time. The fur that adorned the front strap gave them that oomph.

"You just go for the most expensive thing in this store." she complained, coming from the lady with the vintage Chanel purse and loafers to match.

"Come on Mommy, please?" I gave her "the face". It was that same face that she gave into every time.

"Fine! Such a brat, try them on." I smiled and kissed her cheek lightly.

I sat down and untied the laces on my gold Nike Huaraches. I slipped my foot in the sleek shoe.

"Mom, look." She looked up from her phone and smirked.

"I'm only buying them because they are cute." I smiled. That translated to after your ass is done wearing them, they are mine.

"Your father just said your outfit was delivered."

"Thank God, I was getting nervous." I had to rush the order because we were pressed for time. I grabbed the bag and kissed my mom's cheek.

"Seriously, thanks Mommy. I love and appreciate all the things you do for me."

She smiled and kissed my forehead.

"You deserve it baby, I'm so proud of you. You're my world." She wiped the tears from her eyes.

"You got me crying in the street girl, let's go." I smiled.

I remember when we didn't have these luxuries. We've come a long

Calvin

Hey baby,

Happy New Year's Eve, I can't lie and say that you haven't made 2014 the best of my life, thank you baby for your patience and understanding and simply treating me like a queen. I can't wait to bring in 2015 with you tonight, go and get handsome!'

I couldn't help but smile at the text Kelsey sent me. It was shit like this that was making me fall for her.

'Your special you know that right?'

'I've been told, I'm getting my hair done so I'll see you later. I smiled and slid my phone in my back pocket.

"That's my niece you're talking to?" My long time barber also happens to be Kelsey's uncle. He's a couple years older than me so we relate on a lot of different things, but the fact that he's her uncle scares the shit out of me. I mean one slip up and my hair line is gone.

"Man Kordell, don't start." I joked.

He laughed. "You know I'm playing with you, what y'all plan on doing tonight?"

"Leo's son Pierre invited me and Dwayne to his New Year's Eve bash so you know I couldn't pass that up." I tilted my head as he continued cutting my hair.

"I hear it."

"What about you?" I questioned

"Getting my fiancé pregnant" I laughed. If you knew Kordell, you'd know that's just him.

"Yo, you're crazy!"

He laughed and took the cape from around me.

"Alright, you're done."

I stood up and wiped off some of the excess hair off of my pants. I looked in the mirror and admired the precession of the cut.

"Good looks bro, here." I handed him a twenty.

"Nah I'm good, you're family now."

"C'mon, take it man." I tried handing him the twenty.

"No man, you heard me." I dapped him up again.

"Thanks man."

"No problem."

This day can't get any better.

Kelsey

"Mommy, why are you crying?" I asked.

"You look so beautiful."

I smiled and pulled her in for a hug. I must admit, I looked to kill tonight.

The nude Valentino dress complimented my curvaceous body perfectly. My hair was in big barrel curls with a side part. My mother's assistant was gracious enough to do my makeup, nothing extreme though. The doorbell rung and the goosebumps started, I knew it was Calvin.

As soon as I laid eyes on him I wanted to jump on him instantly.

The crisp white dress shirt hung perfectly over his black fitted pants, the fresh pair of Margiela's graced his feet and the simple gold Rolex accompanied his wrist shining. The look I was giving him was the exact same look he was giving me.

"Hey." I spoke low. I was still in a daze from how good he looked.

"Wassup?" He pulled me into a hug and his arms wrapped tightly around my thick waist.

He smelled so fresh and clean. I took in his scent once more.

"Babe, you going to smell me all night?" He let out a throaty laugh.

"No, let's go." he smiled, waved to my parents and led me to the black Escalade parked in my driveway. Aria and Dwayne were already in the back, sucking each other's faces off.

"Ahem, " we both cleared our throats. They jumped back and turned their heads.

"So nasty I swear." I spoke lightly.

"Babe, this is so dope." I said, taking in the ambiance. It was packed in here.

"I know right, but you look better." He looked down at my behind. I blushed lightly.

"Stop, " I smiled.

"I'm serious; you look so good tonight." he whispered in my ear. He looped his arms around my waist.

"Calvin baby?" He began to kiss my neck.

"Hmm?" He grumbled.

"We're in public."

He stopped.

"You right, I made my point anyway." I looked over to see a couple of guys staring in our direction. I shook my head.

"Come, I want you to meet someone."

We walked over and there stood Pierre Stanton. Pierre is the son of an established singer and he's been known to be one of the richer kids in NYC.

Calvin introduced us and he was pretty cool contrary to what I thought he was going to be like. I'm not saying I am filthy rich but I am blessed and so is Calvin so the people that are our ages and rich seem to be rude, arrogant and bossy.

I wondered how Calvin got us in such an exclusive club but now I see. He told me how close they were and how they practically grew up together.

Aria and I mingled with the teen elites of NYC and I must admit it was fun. Everyone was cool and down to earth. I didn't feel a bit nervous.

"Yo, it's a few minutes until the New Year. Y'all grab your bae, boo or whatever and get ready," the DJ spoke into the microphone.

Before I knew it, I was whisked away by Calvin. He grabbed me and kissed my lips sweetly.

"I am so happy that you came into my life. I know that you're that special someone. I might be young but I know that you're meant for me. I promise to continue to treat you like you deserve to be treated so here I am saying in the New Year that I love you."

He placed a small ring on my finger with our initials on it. I couldn't help but tear up, a damn promise ring is great but I love you means much more. I turned to him with tears in my eyes. There wasn't much I could say I was totally speechless.

"I love you too." I managed to say.

I turned my attention to the big projector centered the club and waited for The New Year countdown began.

"5, 4,3,2,1 Happy New Year!" The crowd roared.

We had our first kiss of the New Year and it felt amazing.

A Fool
Kelsey

"Kelsey, your body has been looking good girl what have you been doing?" Aria screamed, gaining attention from everyone in the hallway. I slapped her arm playfully.

"Aria, what is wrong with you?"

"What? I'm just saying Calvin is a lucky man."

I laughed and shook my head.

"What did you get on your math final?" She questioned.

"A 96!" I answered proudly.

She laughed.

"Ha! I got a 97. I told you I was going to get higher than you, where is my $5?" She reached her hand out.

I sighed, "Fine, let me go to my locker."

"Yeah, yeah just make sure I ge-" she gasped.

I looked up from my phone.

"Wha-" I turned my attention to my locker. My hands automatically formed a fist and my blood was boiling. I walked closer to my locker and saw that it was slightly open; my coat lay on the floor. The same coat my mother paid close to $700 for, angry isn't even the word.

I checked my pockets to see if my wallet was still where it was initially. Seeing as though it was, I knew this was nothing more than a malicious target, but whom?

I checked the other pockets and inside was two sonograms; I scanned the small paper trying to read the fine print on the bottom left corner. As soon as I could make out the name on the edge of the paper, I could feel my heart drop, Imani Brinkston.

It was almost like things were moving in slow motion. I

reached for my locker that was slightly open and when I did countless pictures began to fall out. Some were of Calvin and Imani engaging in sexual activities. My mouth fell agape as I could feel the tears stinging my eyes.

How? How could my Calvin, the same Calvin who I shared my deepest darkest insecurities with betray me like this especially with her? I walked away clutching the pictures in my hand tightly.

"Kelsey, wait!"

I could hear Aria call out to me but I ignored her. My mind was someplace else and I was ready for war. This is a feeling I've never had before. I've dealt with enough shade from this girl. I've warned her plenty of times, now she was going to get what she deserved.

I looked around until I spotted Imani leaning against her locker with a smug grin on her face. Her friends surrounded her laughing lightly. She looked down at my hand and then back up at my face.

"I see you got my present." She looked at her nails and then back at me.

In a swift motion, I slapped her with all of my might, creating a loud sound effect that echoed throughout the now full hallway.

"Damn!" I could hear a couple of people say.

Before I knew it, we were rolling on the floor. I used all of my weight and sat on top of her, throwing endless punches to her face. I wanted to stop but I couldn't. I wanted her to feel the pain I felt, the embarrassment. I wasn't going to stop until she begged me to.

"Bitch!" I could hear Aria scream loudly. I'm not sure what was going on but I knew at that moment, she was fighting as well. I could feel strong arms wrap around my waist, pulling me off of Imani's bruised body.

"This is what you wanted right? You earned this ass whooping!" I yelled at her.

"Yo chill!" Calvin yelled.

I pulled away from him and pushed his chest.

"You, don't touch me!" I screamed at him. I rushed out of the school with Calvin hot on my feet.

"Baby, wait up!" He pulled at my arm and I snatched away from him.

"We're done! Do you hear me? Finished! How could you Calvin? I thought your past meant nothing! You got this girl pregnant! Had me looking stupid in front of all of the school. I let you in I-I." At this point, my words stopped flowing. I angrily snatched the promise ring off my finger and tossed it at him, "Go give this to the mother of your child!"

I started to walk away from him but he caught my arm. I snatched away and pushed him, the tears ran down my face uncontrollably and I couldn't stop them. Just when I thought it was okay to remove the guard that stood in front of my heart, this bullshit happens.

Calvin

"Baby, please hear me out." I tried grabbing her arm but she kept snatching away from me, each time rougher than the last.

"No, we are done!" I watched as the tears fell from her eyes and I felt at any moment some would drop from mine.

"Baby." I grabbed her and held her in my arms.

She fought me. She kept pushing me away from her, throwing punches left and right.

"Stop it!" I held her arms so that she couldn't hit me again.

"I hate you!" she yelled out.

I gripped her waist tightly, pulling her towards me.

"Get off of me!" she pushed me roughly but I held her tightly.

"Hear me out Ma please!" I pleaded.

"Fine Calvin, talk." It seemed like once I got a chance to tell her what was up nothing seemed to come out.

"That's exactly what I thought." She snatched away from me and walked towards her car. I knew at that moment I messed up and it would take the Jaws of Life to make this up to her.

I ran my hands over the top of my head, pacing back and forth. My heart was pounding out of my chest and I didn't know what to do.

A few minutes later, Dwayne jogged over to me holding his cheek. I looked at him and asked what happened. Apparently Aria slapped him because she couldn't get to me.

"Man, I don't know what to do." I sat on one of the benches in front of our school.

"I don't know either; she was pissed to the max. I'm not sure how but you have to fix this, bro." I threw my hands on my head and sat on the edge of the bench. What I heard next made me pop my head up almost instantly.

"Tate, where were you?" I could hear Imani whisper.

"My bad, you didn't tell me this shit was going to go down today."

"Well you should've been here while I was taking both of our ass whippings."

I scrunched my face up in confusion.

"Yo, you good?" Dwayne asked me.

"Man, be quiet. Come listen to this." I told him.

He stood behind the brick wall that separated the two of us and listened in.

"You did a good job though! Those sonograms looked so damn real."

"I know man. But you think this is going to break them up for good?"

I shook my head trying to contain myself.

"Yeah, I can finally have my Calvin and you can finally have your Kelsey. Although I don't know why you want her."

"Chill, and shut the fuck up about her."

I clenched my teeth. I couldn't believe these two bastards were actually trying to fuck up my relationship. They are so fucking delusional.

"Yo, you hear this shit?" Dwayne asked me.

I nodded and hopped up off of the bench. My hands were balled up into a fist. These two dumbasses were fucking plotting and this is what they wanted. I don't know why, but they definitely succeeded on fucking Kelsey and I's relationship over.

I was fuming. I was pissed. I hopped off of the seat and stormed around the corner. When they saw me, it looked like they were shitting bricks.

"So this is what the fuck y'all doing?" I walked towards Tate first because I don't hit females. Before I got a chance to knock his shit back, he ran like a bitch leaving Imani there to deal with my anger.

She was shaking and tears were running down her face. Her face was badly bruised from her and Kelsey's fight but I didn't care, did she care when she fucked up my relationship? No!

"You better be fucking happy I don't hit females yo!" I walked towards her but Dwayne pulled me back.

"Bro she's not even worth it, think about Kelsey." I looked at her with the most disgusted look I could muster.

"You right, I need to go and get my *baby* back." I said.

Her face was turning pale and it looked as though she was cringing. That's just what I wanted.

Kelsey

I sat Indian style on my bed crying my eyes out. I was extremely hurt and it felt like my heart was out of my chest. I've been crying almost every day since Calvin and I's big blowout. I slammed the small pillow that I'd been holding in my face and screamed.

I can't lie and say I don't miss Calvin because I do, but at this point my hurt is clouding my better judgement. I pulled my covers back and lay underneath the fresh sheets. I buried my head in between the pillow and comforter and got comfortable. It seems like all I've wanted to do is sleep and stay in my room.

I heard a light tapping on my door and assumed it was my mother. She'd been checking on me nonstop and it is appreciated, however, I just wanted time to myself.

"Who is it?" I asked, sounding muffled.

"Your best friend."

I looked up and smiled slightly.

"Come in." Aria opened the door with a bagful of Chipotle in one hand and a big bag of snacks in the other.

"I come bearing gifts." She sat the bags on top of my mirrored dresser and sat on the edge of my bed. I smiled lightly.

"Thank you." She kicked off her shoes and came to lie next to me.

"Poor baby." She looked at the puddle of tissues that surrounded me.

"Ari', it hurts so badly." I confessed and broke down.

She hugged me tightly.

"I know it does but sitting in here all day won't help anything, why don't you call him?" I looked at her with the most grimacing look I could make up.

"Alright fine, but I'm telling you, it'll help if you just talk it out with him. He could be feeling the same way."

"Fuck his feelings." I yelled out.

"Okay, alright, relax." She said while sitting up.

"I'm sorry. I'm just so pissed like I want to punch him in the face, Aria. How could you have sex with that thing?" I sat up and reached for the bag of Chipotle.

"That's why you need to talk to him and figure that out, clear the air."

She reached in the bag for her burrito. I sat on the bed taking in what she was saying. Maybe I should answer his calls and maybe we should meet up but my anger just wouldn't let me.

"I'll think about it." I said plainly while eating my quesadilla.

I wanted to talk to Calvin, but I was in no rush to do so. I still needed to calm myself down because I was still pissed and afraid of what I may say to him when I see him.

Reconciliation

Calvin

I tossed the small football up and down while I lie on my bed. These last couple of days I've been miserable, and only because my baby hasn't been answering my phone calls or speaking to me.

I'm not about to lie and say that I haven't been losing sleep over her because I have. I just wanted to hold and kiss her and tell her what the deal really was but she wasn't giving me a chance too.

I laid there for a while until my cell phone began to vibrate. I grabbed it off of the charger and noticed it was a text from Kelsey.

Meet me at the pier I looked at the text and couldn't help but smile. Even though she wasn't feeling me right now, I was happy she finally wanted to speak to me.

'Cool.' I texted back and grabbed a pair of sweats off of the couch in my room. I'm not sure how this was going to play out but I'm ready for it all.

As soon as I pulled up to the pier, I saw my baby looking good as ever. The black Nike tights she wore hugged her thick thighs and the Nike cool fit sweatshirt she wore fit her kind of snug.

I know my mind should be on repairing whatever's been broken but I had to admire her for a while. She was in deep thought; I could tell by the way she was staring at the water.

"Hey." I said low. She turned and looked at me. Her hair was pulled out of her face showing her natural beauty.

"Hi." She turned to face me.

There was a brief silence so I decided to speak.

"I miss you."

She rolled her eyes and looked away. I moved closer to her.

"Don't act like that baby."

"How am I supposed to act, Calvin? You got this girl pregnant and I'm supposed to be happy?" She said yelling.

"Baby, I really don't want to do the screaming, can we just talk?" I said trying to calm her down.

"Fine Calvin, let's talk." She shifted her weight to one leg and placed her hands on her hip.

"Later that day I overheard Imani and Tate. They set all this shit up for us to break up."

She scrunched her face up and looked at me confused.

"Why?" I looked at her.

"They want us to be with them. They figured if they did this, we'd break up and we'd be with them. Its crazy baby, but you have to believe me."

"But the sonograms."

"Tate made fake ones. I don't know how, but he did."

She gasped and looked at me.

"If something like that really happened I would've told you right away. We did sleep together but that was before me and you dated. I promise you it meant nothing." She stared at me for a minute and walked over to where I was standing.

"Are you attracted to her?" She asked.

"Hell no."

"Do you love me?" She asked.

"Yes, with everything in me." We were chest to chest but our hands stayed to the side. She reached up and caressed my cheek. And then slapped me with all of her might.

"Then don't lie to me like that, feeding me that bullshit ass lie. I'm supposed to believe that crazy ass story?" She said while her chest heaved up and down.

"Yo, you just put your hands on me?!" I asked, stunned.

"Yeah I did because you're lying and then left out the whole part where y'all were texting. You thought I wouldn't find out?" She said while crossing her arms over her chest.

"You put your hands on me." I said again while holding my face.

I looked at her. Even though I loved her, I was pissed the fuck off. She put her hands on me and for no reason. I looked at her for a minute and shook my head.

"I'm leaving." I walked towards my car, leaving her standing there alone.

"Wait!" She grabbed my arm and I yanked away from her.

"No, what you just did was mad fucking disrespectful! I don't have any reason to lie. I came here and told you the fucking truth and you put your hands on me! That's not cool yo."

I walked towards my car slammed the door and then pulled off. I really thought this was going to be the time we hashed it out and dead this, instead the tables turned and I was the pissed one.

Kelsey

"I can't believe I did that." I said to myself while pacing back and forth.

I don't know what came over me, but whatever it was, it was strong. I never intended for Calvin and me to get into it this bad but I felt like he was lying because that story sounded so made up. That was until Aria called and told me what Dwayne told her about the situation and it was the exact same story Calvin had told me.

I felt terrible and I needed to apologize ASAP although it was virtually impossible to get in touch with him. He wasn't answering any of my calls or texts. I knew at that moment that I pissed him off. I sighed and sat back on my couch. I really did it this time, man. In a matter of minutes the tables had flipped and I was on the wrong side.

Peace Offering

Kelsey

"Hello." Calvin answered groggily.

"Can you please come over?" I asked.

He sighed for a minute and then agreed.

"Fine." He hung up without saying goodbye.

A couple of minutes passed and a knocking on the door brought me out of my thoughts. I already knew it was Calvin. I straightened my clothes out and opened the door. He examined my body and then looked at my face.

"Come in."

He followed behind me and sat on the leather love seat across from the couch I was sitting on.

"Why are you so far?" I asked.

"I'm not trying to get slapped again." He said while staring directly at me.

"Calvin, I really am sorry. It was just my mind was in another place. I should've never put my hands on you it was just, I-I." I could feel the tears well up in my eyes.

"I didn't like the thought of someone being with you. I don't care if it was before me or after me, I don't like it. In my mind, she got a piece of you that was mine." I wiped my eyes.

"Come here." He said low.

I got up and walked towards where he was now standing.

"I'm nobody else's but yours baby. You need to understand that."

I nodded as he took the pads of his thumb to wipe my excess tears.

"Believe that."

Calvin

I pulled her into my lap.

"I'm sorry, I should've told you, and I didn't, forgive me please. This is what Imani wants, for you to leave me, please don't do that. I miss you so much, it's almost like I'm empty without you."

She wrapped her arms around my neck and kissed me, it caught me off guard. Our heads bobbed back and forth.

She turned so that she was straddling me. My hands roamed up and down her back as we continued to exchange hungry kisses.

I needed to stop myself. She was not ready and at the rate we were going, that was all about to go out the window.

"Baby, stop." I tried to stop her kisses, but they were getting more and more aggressive.

"Kelsey baby, stop before we do something we can't do."

"Why can't we?" She asked.

I was shocked at her response. It wasn't what I was expecting at all.

"So what you want me to do baby?" I groaned.

She licked my neck and up to my ear.

"I want you to eat it."

I damn near choked.

"You sure?"

She nodded slowly and got off of me. She took my hand and

led me upstairs to her bedroom.

"Lay down," I instructed her.

She did as I asked. I took my shirt off and threw it down. I hovered over her and kissed her gently.

"You sure you want me to do this?" I asked again.

She nodded and kissed me back.

I pulled at the hem of her shirt and lifted it up slowly. I wanted to see all of her every inch, I pulled it off of her and tossed it across the room, I kissed her neck and then kissed down to her breasts. I reached back behind her and unsnapped her bra.

I was praying my dumbass didn't mess it up. I watched as they fell slightly out of the bra. I took each one in my mouth and sucked on it lightly, I heard her moan.

I licked down to her stomach and kissed everything, every roll, every stretch mark. I continued to kiss down to the waistband of her panties. I pulled them off and stuck them in my pocket. I observed her body and its beauty.

"Open your legs baby." I looked down at her. It was beautiful, just as beautiful as her body. She was dripping; I bent down and kissed her slit. I used my tongue to open her lips up; I went back to kissing her inner thighs and then back down. I licked around her clit and then attacked it viciously. She moaned, wrapped her legs around my neck and pulled at my hair.

"Mm C-Calvin!"

That's all the encouragement I needed, "How does it feel baby?"

"Good, so good!"

She could barely get the words out. I continued to suck her dry, until she screamed and her sweet juices covered my lips. I looked up at her and watched as her eyelids got heavier and heavier. I smiled to myself, I put her to sleep.

Forgiveness

Calvin

She lay in my arms sleeping so peacefully. I mean damn she's beautiful but she's even prettier when she's sleep. The vibration of my phone interrupted me from staring at her. I looked at the caller I.D and saw it was Dwayne, I told him I was coming over there to talk.

"Wassup, how'd it go?"

"It went good, she's sleeping right now"

"I knew y'all asses weren't going to stay mad at each other. I'm just happy you're good, you were starting to worry me." It was true, I had been bugging out these last couple of days, I was going through the motions. I was mad, sad then happy. I was just acting like a female.

"Yeah I'm cool now, I got her back."

"That's good, but swing by the gym. I want to play ball."

"Alright, don't have me waiting."

"Shut up I'll be there."

I hung up. "Baby, " I kissed her cheek lightly.

"Hmm?" She held on to me a little tighter.

"I'm about to go."

"Why, I want you to stay." she mumbled.

"I'll be back tomorrow so we could do something, I promise." She nodded and let me up. I walked to her bathroom and took a minute to look around. Kelsey really is a lady, everything was so neat.

"You have an extra toothbrush babe?"

"Yeah, in the medicine cabinet."

I looked up and grabbed it.

I heard her shuffling around in the bedroom.

"Calvin, where are my underwear?"

I smiled and patted my pants pocket, "I don't know baby, did you look in the bed?"

"Yeah, whatever. I'm about to shower anyway, I'll put on fresh ones."

I turned off the faucet and grabbed a clean towel to wipe off my face and walked out of the bathroom.

"Where are you going now?" I grabbed my t-shirt and put it over my head.

"To go play some ball with Dwayne." I turned to face her.

She bit her bottom lip lightly.

"Why you looking at me like that?"

She smiled, "No reason."

I smiled at her and slid my hoodie over my head.

"It's alright to admire your man."

She sucked her teeth. I laced up my sneakers and walked towards her. I bent down so we were face to face, "Thank you for giving me another chance."

She grabbed both sides of my face and pecked my lips, "You're forgiven baby."

I kissed her back.

"I love you yo."

She smiled. "I love you too."

"Before I go baby, give me your hand." I slid the promise ring on her finger.

"Now it's back where it's supposed to be."

She smiled and looked down at it.

"It's so pretty. I never realized its beauty until it was gone, I guess I missed it"

"Yeah now never take it off." She looked up at me.

"Don't give me a reason to."

"I won't, I swear. I won't."

Kelsey

"Girl, he put me out!"

"Eeeee, girl it was that good?" Aria questioned.

"You don't even know, it was so good my ass couldn't find my panties."

"Oh my God!" Aria giggled.

"Yes, if I wasn't in love then, then I definitely am now."

"You're crazy, guess who I saw though?"

"Who?"

"Imani's ass."

I rolled my eyes just at the mention of her name.

"Eww," I laid on the edge of my bed.

"I know, she came in my mom's boutique, her eye is messed up!"

"What did she say?"

"Nothing, as soon as she saw me she rushed to put on her shades, then she had the nerve to be loud about how much money she has but then her credit card declined."

"Damn."

"That's not it, my mom's employee ran it through the system about three more times and it still didn't go through. The kicker is her father Councilman Brinkston is being brought up on embezzlement charges in Federal court. After her card got denied once more she ran out of the store."

"God, she can't catch a break."

"You know what, as horrible of a person that girl is, I feel bad for her."

"Me too."

I genuinely felt bad for her, but she has a lot to learn about treating people and most importantly herself.

"Girl, let me call you back, Calvin's on the other line."

"Okay, I'm probably going to hit the sheets girl, I'm beat."

"Okay love you, bye."

"Love you too boo." I clicked over and Calvin's deep voice answered.

"Wassup babe?" He spoke.

"Hey."

"I just wanted to tell you that I'm home from the gym."

"Okay, let me let you go, I know you're tired."

"I am, I'll come scoop you up tomorrow and take you out to eat or something."

"Okay see you then, love you."

"Love your scary ass too, give me a kiss."

I gave him a kiss through the phone and ended the call.

I'd be lying if I said I didn't miss him, but I have him back now and that's all that matters.

Acceptance

Kelsey

These last couple of weeks had been so stressful. It's like every time I want a social life, the college process comes along and snatches that idea right away. A person my age wouldn't dare be in a Starbucks trying to get just a little peace.

Today is the day I'll find out if I've been accepted into Columbia University or not and I needed to just have a few minutes alone. The vibration of my phone interrupted my thoughts.

It's here baby girl come open it!

I could feel my stomach get queasy, my palms began to sweat. This moment determined everything from this point on my life, my future, Calvin.

Calvin

"Open it baby, just open it," my mother and father encouraged me.

I blew out a breath and ripped the envelope open.

I unfolded the paper and began to read the letter,

Calvin Powers, On behalf of the faculty and staff of The University of Los Angeles we would like to congratulate you on your acceptance as a member of the Class of 2019!

A single tear fell down my face, I couldn't even talk. This is what I've been busting my ass for. UCLA is one of the best when it comes down to college football, it felt like I was one step closer to going pro.

"You did it baby. All the hard work, dedication and perseverance you've put forth. You're getting the reward now."

"Man, I'm so proud of you, I can't." I knew that voice that was that I'm trying not to cry because I'm a real one voice.

"I know Pops, I did it for you."

And I did, he's been my inspiration since I've been a baby. Yeah he messes up, but who doesn't?

This is who I did it for, my family. As soon as I settled my thoughts, it all settled in. I'd have to leave Kelsey. We both talked about it, but now that it's set in stone we definitely have to talk about it. I don't know how, but we have to. I'm not ready, I'm not.

Mixed Feelings

Kelsey

I jumped up and down into my jeans trying to get my butt in them.

I'm not sure what's been going on with my hips lately but they've been spreading out of control, it's probably all of the eating Calvin and I had been doing. A smile spread across my face.

I looked over my phone and saw Calvin's text message.

I'm downstairs waiting for you baby.

I smiled lightly and sent him a quick reply.

I'll be down in a few.

I slid my feet in my olive colored UGGS that matched my winter coat perfectly.

I gave myself another once over and then walked downstairs.

"Mommy and Daddy, I'll be back Calvin and I are going to grab some breakfast."

My dad turned his head from the newspaper and looked in my direction.

"Baby girl, you and I were supposed to go to the Rutgers Girls' basketball game."

I felt like crap. I feel like I've been slipping up when it came to my dad's and I relationship.

"I promise Daddy, I'll make it up to you." I kissed his forehead, and then my mom's cheek.

Calvin's eyes were so busy in his phone that he didn't realize I walked out.

I tapped on the window lightly. He hopped out and walked towards me.

"My bad baby." He kissed me lightly and opened my door.

"Where are we going?" I asked.

"Let's go do something fun." He plugged the AUX cord up to his phone.

"Like what?" I questioned.

He turned to face me.

"I don't, but before we do anything, let's go grab something to eat. A nigga is starving."

"You're not the only one," I said truthfully.

I watched as Calvin rapped along to J.Cole's *"Love Yours"*

From what Calvin's told me he has been a fan of J.Cole's since before the hype.

"Babe, what are you getting me for my birthday?"

"Calvin, if you ask me what I'm getting you again, I'm not going to get you anything."

Calvin's been pestering me about his birthday gift for a minute now and it's getting annoying.

"Who you talking to?" He asked.

"You, you've been bothering me about your gift since December, babe it's annoying."

"Don't worry; when your birthday comes up don't ask for a

hint. Matter of fact, I'm not getting your ass shit!"

I rolled my eyes, "Alright, Alright!" I whined.

"Nah, don't ask for anything."

"Baby!" I bargained.

"Give me a kiss and I'll reconsider."

I smiled and kissed his neck. I licked up to his ear and then kissed his cheek.

"I'm back in your good graces now?"

"Yeah I'll let it slide for now."

I side eyed him.

"Alright Calvin, shut up now!"

He smiled lightly and then pulled into IHOP's parking lot.

"I'm starving." Calvin said while opening my door.

"Me too." I walked inside.

We ordered and waited for our food. I watched Calvin from the corner of my eyes. I was so blessed to have a boyfriend that's so fine, so good to me. It's almost surreal. It's going to hurt so bad when we go away to college.

"Baby, you good?" Calvin grabbed my hands from across the table and kissed them.

"I'm fine." I sipped my orange juice. He stared at me for a while and then decided to speak. He cleared his throat first and then spoke.

"I got accepted to UCLA."

I knew already, I knew we'd eventually have to split but it felt so wrong. I swallowed the lump in my throat and I could feel the tears at the brim of my eyes. Don't cry; suck it up; he's going to live

156

out his dreams, whether they're with you or without you.

"Babe that's great, I'm so proud of you, I have to tell you some big news too."

"You got into Columbia? He asked.

"Yeah, I found out yesterday." I tucked a strand of hair behind my ears.

"I'm not about to lie to you, I don't want you to go." His tone was serious.

"I don't want you to go to UCLA either but we've worked hard for this babe. We get to live out our dreams. UCLA and Columbia do that for us"

"You right baby, I understand. I really do, it's just going to be hard." He looked into my eyes.

"Let's not talk about it, let's just focus on us being together now."

"You right, I love you." I smiled.

"I love you too Calvin, always will."

Yeah I'm happy for us, but it's hard to enjoy it knowing our days are numbered. Let's just make the best out of it.

Quality Time

Kelsey

I couldn't help but gasp at the beautiful spread in front of me, the ambiance of the restaurant was to die for overwhelming to be exact. I couldn't help but tear up. This must've took so much time and effort

"Why are you crying?" He asked.

"It's just all too much babe, you give me too much." I fell into his chest and began to cry harder. The real reason I was such a mess was thinking about the fact of him leaving me began eating away at the surface. I tried to focus on positive thoughts but I couldn't because I always reflected back onto my love for him and how much I'll miss him.

"Babe, is this not what you wanted?"

I shook my head.

"Not at all babe, it's amazing. I'm just going to miss it all when we leave for school."

I could hear him sigh.

"We talked about this already Ma. We have to cherish the time we have together and if that means by making you feel like a queen then I'll do so, but this sad shit have to go."

I looked up at him and he used the pads of his thumbs to wipe my tears away.

"I know." I sniffled.

"So can we enjoy the rest of this night and the rest of these months?" he asked.

"Yes," I smiled lightly and kissed the tip of his nose.

"Now, let's eat." We walked through the empty restaurant.

"Calvin, where are the people?" I asked.

"I rented it out." My eyes widened.

"Cousare! Calvin, are you crazy it's so expensive in here?"

It's no secret that both Calvin and I are somewhat of Heir's and Heiress' but sometimes Calvin goes overboard with the gifts. He laughed instantly.

"Babe, relax and sit your ass down." I rolled my eyes and sat down. After pushing in my chair, he did the same. I looked down at the special menu.

"Calvin, do you realize we act like grown ass people?"

He smiled and put his menu down.

"To be honest, this is what I always wanted."

"Yeah me too, but not this young. You don't think we overdo it?" he smirked, showing those bottom golds that I adored on him.

"I don't care what people think of us. If they think we overdo it then they're jealous and bitter."

I smiled lightly.

Calvin honestly didn't care what others thought of our relationship and he made that very obvious. I was plastered all on his Instagram and he was a huge fan of PDA. I loved every moment of it.

"Even though I told you this a million times today babe, Happy Birthday!"

He smiled.

"Thank you baby," I reached under the table and grabbed his gift. I'd literally went everywhere trying to get this gift and I was anxious to see his reaction, maybe too anxious.

"After dinner babe," I looked at him and scrunched up my face.

"After you damn near kicked me out of your car for not telling you what I got you, you better open this gift." He laughed.

"No babe, after dinner."

I rolled my eyes. "You mad at me?"

I playfully ignored him.

"Come over here."

"Nope," I popped the p.

"Yeah, all I know is you better come over here."

I smiled, got up and walked towards him. He pulled me into his lap and placed his large hands on my thighs; he looked down and gripped them. This is something he enjoyed doing. Little did he know it was sending me into a frenzy.

"Why you mad? " he spoke huskily. All the while his hands traveled upward.

"I-I'm not mad."

He sucked on my neck roughly.

"C-Calvin you're going to leave a mark, s-stop"

I bit my lip lightly as he continued the vicious assault on my neck. I dipped my head back as he continued to grip my thighs

160

tightly. I felt him stop.

"That's for being rude, go sit down."

I opened my eyes and hit him on his chest lightly.

"You're an ass, I swear." I got up and walked back towards my chair. I could hear him laughing.

"Keep laughing Calvin and I'm leaving." He still continued to laugh so I pretended to get up and go, not before he pulled me back down. I wasn't going anywhere and he knew that, we ate laughed and talked up until the last minute.

"Now, I know your ass is thirsty to see your gift, so here."

I threw my napkin at him as he handed me three big bags.

I handed him his gift and before I could say what he meant to me, he ripped it to shreds. Leaving the Balenciaga box in the open, he opened the box but instead of seeing his 17th pair sneakers, he saw an envelope filled with two tickets and backstage passes to meet his idol, J. Cole. His face was priceless!

He let out a loud scream and kissed me repeatedly.

"I fucking love you girl!"

I smiled and kissed him back.

I opened my first gift and nearly fell to the floor.

"A Rolex!"

He smiled and encouraged me to open the rest of the gifts. I was so stuck on the Rolex that I couldn't process the Givenchy flats and purse to match. I jumped into his arms and wrapped my legs around his waist.

"You're the best baby, thank you." I kissed him with everything in me, damn near knocking the wind out of myself. He gripped my butt firmly.

Aria

Dwayne, your asleep?" I fingered his curls and tugged at them lightly.

"No, just thinking." he answered huskily.

"About what?"

"Us."

I raised an eyebrow, "What about?"

"I mean you don't like titles, but what are we?"

I was hesitant. After Chris, I'd been standoffish when it came to relationships. He turned around and grabbed me so that I was straddling him.

"I'm trying Dwayne, I really am. I just don't feel I'm over Chris fully yet." He sighed and moved me off of his lap. He grabbed his coat and walked towards the door.

"Dwayne, can you just listen?" I couldn't believe he was acting this way. He kept walking until I grabbed the end of his jacket.

"I told you don't bring him up and that's what the fuck you do. Let me ask you a question, how long am I going to have to wait? I put in the work. I was there when he wasn't, now I have to wait because of him!"

I couldn't help but feel like crap.

"Dwayne, please real-" I grabbed his arm but he snatched it

back.

"No I'm good. When you ready to give me what I've given you, then call me." He walked over and kissed my forehead before walking out. I couldn't even think straight.

Chris had hindered every aspect of my life. The only way to fully get over him was to confront him because I can't risk losing Dwayne.

I plopped down on my bed and sighed, if it isn't one thing it's another.

Calvin

"Yo, you're crazy!" I looked over at Kelsey who rapped along to Drake's *Legend*. She really thought she was doing something.

"I'm the youngest nigga' repping!" she screamed out.

I shook my head and stopped the recording.

"Why are you laughing at me babe? Your dad might consider signing me."

I laughed and shook my head. Her laughing died down but her smile was still wide, damn she's so perfect.

I looked over at her wrist, observing the watch I brought her.

"I take it you like your gift?"

She smiled, "I love it babe, thank you." She rubbed my thigh lightly.

I looked down at her hand and then back at the road. I learned to love the smaller things about her, like how she carried herself. Her nails were always done, her hair was too. She always smelled good and she always matched my fly. Those small things drive me crazy.

"Baby I'm nervous," she whined.

"For what? You've met my family already." Today was my cousin's fifth birthday and I brought Kelsey knowing how much my family loved her.

"Yeah, but your aunt doesn't. She made that very clear." She rolled her eyes.

"Cut it out Ma, my aunt's a little difficult with everybody, that's just her."

"Yeah, I guess." I pulled into the skating rink's parking lot. I turned to face her.

"You know I got you, stop worrying." I grabbed her chin and kissed her lips. She reached up and wiped some of her lip gloss off of my lips.

"I know babe." I kissed her lips once more and then got out.

As soon as we walked in, I spotted my family instantly. It's a lot of us and we were the loudest. Before I could walk in any further my Uncle Lee stopped me.

"Damn," I said low. You know that one uncle that talks too much and it's always about nothing, that's Lee.

"My man, look at you boy. You're doing big things now, I see." he looked over at Kelsey. She gripped my hand tightly.

"Yeah, where's Auntie Leah?" I cut the conversation short trying to avoid talking even more.

"She's over there with the kids." I nodded and grabbed Kelsey's hand.

"Baby, slow down," she whispered.

"My bad baby." We walked over towards my aunt and cousins who made it their business to stare her down every time I bring her around, especially my younger cousins.

"Hey Kelsey," they all said together. They didn't even greet me; they just went straight to my girl. I thought we were family.

"Kelsey!" I heard a small voice scream. I turned to see my smaller cousin running towards Kelsey.

"Hey pretty girl! Happy Birthday!" Kelsey handed Kayla my cousin her gift.

"Thank you so much! Want to skate?" she stuttered a bit.

"Sure thing; let me take off my coat and go get a pair of skates and I'll skate with the birthday girl all day." She bent down to kiss her cheek, giving me a clear view of her ass.

I smiled and bit my bottom lip, but before I could enjoy it, I earned a slap to the back of my head. I turned my head, ready to slap one of my cousins, only to see me Leah, my aunt.

"Hey Auntie," I rubbed the back of my neck and smiled lightly.

"Uh-huh, I saw your little nasty behind. Go with your cousins, I want to talk to Kelsey."

"Alright Auntie, please be easy on her."

She rolled her eyes and sighed, "Y'all acting like I hate the girl, I just had to feel her out. I'm fine now." I shook my head and walked to where my cousins were.

"Damn, how you pull that?" one of my cousins screamed out.

I stuck my middle finger up and put our coats on one of the spare chairs.

"Don't start none of y'all!" I sat down prepared for them to bust my balls all night about Kelsey.

Kelsey

I swallowed hard when I spotted Calvin's aunt walking towards me. When I first met her, I thought she was beyond beautiful. Her smooth brown skin and perfect figure intrigued me, that was until she gave me the third degree.

"Hey Ms. Kayla, can I borrow your best friend?" she cooed.

"Yep Mama, I'm going to eat pizza." She gave a toothy smile and ran off, we both laughed.

"Sit down Miss."

I swallowed the lump in my throat and sat down.

"I first want to say I'm sorry for how I acted at dinner. I'm just very protective over my nephews, they're like my babies. Calvin has a lot going for him and gold diggers look at him and automatically see shoes and purses."

"I understand, however, that's not me. I genuinely love Calvin for Calvin."

"Love?" she questioned.

"Yes, love." she smiled.

"It seems as though Calvin feels the same. I know you're a sweet girl, I just had to test the waters." I smiled and let out a breath. She leaned in and hugged me.

It felt good that someone besides ourselves saw the love we had for each other. This could be forever. You never know!

A Sit Down

Aria

I tapped my fingers against the table awaiting Chris's arrival; I had agreed to meet with him so we could talk.

I sipped my lemon water and looked towards the entrance. I was finally ready to get this over with. If I wanted to pursue anything with Dwayne, I had to finish things officially with Chris. I looked down at my phone and then at the entrance, I was growing impatient with every minute that passed.

It was typical Chris to be late. 20 minutes later he strolled through the semi-empty diner like he owned it. He walked towards me and slid in the booth.

"What's up, miss me?" he spoke confidently.

I rolled my eyes, unamused by his antics. "Not at all."

His smile faded, "So why am I here?"

"I feel I need to get some stuff of my chest, Christian"

Before I could continue, he pulled his phone out and began texting.

That's when I realized all of the feelings I once had all vanished, how could I have ever been attracted to him?

I laughed lightly.

"You know what Christian? I came here because I felt I needed to clear a few things up with you before I jumped into a relationship with someone who is more than a man than your ass could have ever been. I thought that maybe I had some sort of love for you still, but today I realize I don't even have an ounce. You don't deserve me and I'm so happy I didn't give you my prized possession because I'm afraid your ass wouldn't have known what to do with it. From this day forward, don't call me or text me. I'm completely done. Goodbye Christian." I slid out of the booth and rushed out.

I needed to catch Dwayne and I knew just the place he'd be.

Dwayne

"That's right y'all hustle." I screamed.

On the weekends my dad signed me up to volunteer at this football camp for kids nine to fourteen. At first, I was pissed. I mean every Saturday *here*, but I've grown to love doing this.

"Can we go get some water, please?" one of the kids begged.

I laughed lightly.

"Yeah, y'all go get some Gatorade on the back tables." I turned and there she stood smiling.

I can't lie and say I haven't missed Aria because I did. She signaled for me to come over. I sighed and walked towards her.

"I'll be back, y'all start running laps."

As soon as I got close to her I couldn't help but want to kiss her lips. She smiled but I tried to keep my facial expression straight.

"Can we talk?"

I nodded. We went to sit on the small benches outside of the gymnasium.

"Hey," she said shyly.

"Wassup?" I tried to sound unfazed.

"Listen Dwayne, I've been thinking about what you've said and I realize my wrongs. I know you feel I haven't given you all of me because you think Chris still holds a piece, and to be honest, he does"

I sighed, "Yo, not this shit again." I started to get up but she pulled me back down.

"Listen to me Dwayne, please."

I sat back down.

"Now yes, he has a little piece of me but you have so much more of me. You have all of me. The piece of me he has is the old immature Aria who lost herself in a really bad situation. You have the new Aria, the one who's willing to give herself to you fully. "She stopped and I watched the tears roll down her face and I dried them with my hands.

"Why are you crying?"

She looked up at me and said softly, "I feel like I hurt you and that wasn't my intention."

I pulled her into my lap, "I'm sorry, alright."

She looked at me, "For what?" she asked.

"I should've let you talk. I was so mad babe; all I wanted was to be with you. I later realized I can't rush everything."

She smiled and kissed the tip of my nose, "I'm sorry too, for bringing him up. I was wrong too."

I reached up and kissed her lips, "It's cool I'm over it."

She smiled and kissed me, "I don't want to fight again," she said though a laugh.

"Yep, only if we make up after" I gripped her thighs lightly and smirked.

"You're so nasty," she rolled her eyes.

I smiled. I finally got my baby, all of her.

Rejoice

Kelsey

"So when am I going to be able to meet your little friend?" my aunt asked.

"If you came to church then you would've met him."

She rolled her eyes and threw a magazine at me.

"What?"

My flight was long and I was tired. I always admired my aunt and her ambition. She took the plus size modeling world by storm when she modeled in Alexander Wang's fashion show. She then took the entire fashion world by storm when she later released her collaboration with him.

We've always had a connection. I think it's because of how close we are in age. She's only 6 years older than me so we have a couple of things in common.

"You're such a drama queen, but you'll meet him today. He's going to come over."

She smiled, "I can't wait! Has your Grandmother met him before today?"

"Yeah, she thinks he's the best."

"*My mother* thinks he's the best?"

"Yep, she said he reminds her of Granddaddy."

"Really, then I definitely need to meet him"

"What about you?" I asked.

"Me what?" She tried to hide her smile.

"I saw on TMZ the other day that you were spotted leaving Nanos with Branden!" I screamed playfully and she began to blush.

"I don't know what you're talking about." She picked up the magazine and began to flip through.

"Auntie Mia, you don't even believe that."

She smiled, "Branden is nothing more than a friend." She smiled and bit her bottom lip.

Branden Lawrence played as a Denver Nugget in the NBA and he is gorgeous!

"The tabloids might believe that, but your niece who knows you doesn't."

"What I'm about to tell you can't say a thing, not even to your mother." I took my fingers and zipped them over my lips.

"We've been dating."

I gasped and slapped my hand over my mouth, "How?" I asked.

"I met him at NYFW and from then on it kind of just grew into something more."

I smiled, "Did you guys have…?" I tilted my head.

"That's none of your business." By the smirk on her face I already had my answer.

"Do you know how lucky you are?" I asked.

"The question is, does he?"

"Yes Auntie!" I loved her confidence. It dripped off of her; I could feel the vibration from my phone.

I'm here babe.

I smiled, "He's here, and I'll be back."

I grabbed my coat and walked downstairs. I hope he doesn't feel ambushed; all of my family come to Grandmother's to eat Sunday dinner.

"Gigi, I'll be back, Calvin's here."

"Why didn't you tell me he was coming? I didn't make his red velvet cake."

I scrunched my face up.

"You didn't ask if I wanted cake."

She rolled her eyes

"I see you all the time girl, go on."

I put on a fake pout and walked out of the house. Calvin's matte black Audi sat in the driveway while he occupied the hood.

"Hey babe." I kissed his lips, but strangely he didn't kiss me back. I also noticed he didn't change out of his church clothes.

"What's wrong?" I asked.

"Nothing."

"Calvin, what's wrong?"

"Man, I just got some news."

I looked up at him and he avoided contact.

"What happened baby?"

He hesitated for a few seconds.

"I have to go to my college; the coach of the football team wants to talk to me."

"That sounds good, why do you sound so sad?"

He sighed, "I have to go May 11th."

"That's my birthday."

"I know babe, I'm sorry. I tried to reschedule but the admissions office wasn't having it."

On the inside I felt horrible, but I know Calvin's career was more important than anything.

"It's okay; we could probably do something when you come back." I didn't think I'd sound as disappointed as I did.

"Nah, that's not good enough baby." He pulled me by my waist. "I wanted to spend it with you though."

I smiled and kissed his lips lightly.

"Babe I'm fine, I promise."

"Yeah, but I'm not." He looked away and poked his cheek with his tongue.

I turned his face back to me. "Listen I'm fine, I promise.

He sighed.

"Let's go in to eat, its cold." I pulled his arm and walked ahead of him.

As soon as we walked in, my family greeted him, but there was one person who I really wanted him to meet.

"Auntie Mia!" I called out to her. She came almost too quickly.

"That's your aunt?" He asked.

I laughed lightly and nodded.

"Hmm, 34 inch slim fit Amani suit, nice." She extended her hand and he shook it.

"How'd you know that?"

She laughed.

"I'm a fashion designer honey; I've been trained to know these things. Now y'all come with me to the family room; I want to talk to you both."

I sighed. This was definitely not what I was expecting. She's the cool aunt, we sat down and my aunt went right into it.

"Now, I know you are two young attractive adults and I know sex is on y'all mind."

I put my hand to my head and turned away from her.

"Don't play Kelsey; you know what I'm hip to. Now as I was saying, sex is probably the topic of conversation. I just hope protection is used." Calvin began coughing.

"You need some water?" my aunt asked.

"Nah, I'm good." I rubbed circles on his back.

"Are you guys having sex?"

"Auntie!"

"What, I need to know."

"I'm still a virgin, so no."

She sighed.

"That's good, Calvin are you good to my niece?"

"I mean I'd like to say I am, I hope I am." He looked over at me and I couldn't help but smile.

"Now Calvin, you probably think I'm crazy and I am, especially over my niece but I think you're a nice young man so you won me over."

He smiled, "Thank you."

"No problem, if I didn't like you I wouldn't of wasted my time, but I was waiting for you at the door." She tilted her head and we all laughed.

"Auntie, can we go eat?"

"Yeah let's go. I'm starving."

I'm just happy my aunt approved. That small little conversation we just had got my mind off of Calvin not being with me for my birthday. I was just wondering how long this was going to last.

Shocked

Kelsey

I was so deep into my book I didn't realize who had sat across from me.

Sure it was a public place, but there were plenty of empty seats. Why sit by me? I lifted my head to see who it was and without hesitation I grabbed my Cafe vanilla bean Frappuccino and was ready to leave.

"Wait, can I please talk to you?"

I looked at him like he was crazy, "Tate, you need to get away from me." I gathered the rest of my things.

"Please before you go, just know I'm sorry."

I looked at him as if he was crazy.

"I don't need an apology; I need for you to move."

"Please man! It's been eating me up. I wasn't raised to put my hands on women and I needed to apologize."

"So you want to apologize because you feel guilty?"

"No, because it wasn't right. I'll continue to stay away from you. I just need to know I'm forgiven."

I scrunched my face up. I'm not sure what had gotten into him, but we were never close enough for him to feel like this. I did feel an ounce of sympathy. He looked terrible.

"I was brought up to forgive, even for people's simple-minded actions." I walked towards the exit.

"Calvin's lucky," he spoke low.

I shook my head, "No, I believe I am."

I left him there. I'm not sure why Tate was so strongly affected by his actions, it could be guilt. Whatever it may be, I accepted his apology now. As long as he didn't get this misconstrued, friendship isn't in the near future. This was just an acceptance of an apology, nothing more and nothing less.

All I could do was sigh. I had finally after hours of trying to take a proper nap drifted off to sleep but yet another interruption came.

"Hello." I answered without looking at the caller I.D.

"Yo, come outside."

I looked away from my phone and then back at it again, "Calvin?"

I didn't recognize his voice, he sounded harsh and angry.

"Yeah, come."

Before I could say anything, the end clicked indicating he had hung up. I rolled my eyes and got up.

I'd been walking around in joggers and a sweatshirt all day and my hair was wrapped in a doobie.

I had no desire to get cute so I slid my feet in my fringed Hunter boots and threw on my long Montclair coat.

I looked at the small white snowflakes that began to collect on Calvin's Audi. I wonder how long he's been here.

I slid into the sleek leather seats and closed the door, "Hey baby."

"Wassup?" He scrolled through his phone.

"I like these pop-up visits." I smiled lightly but Calvin didn't. His face remained stale.

"Why I got to hear from people you having lunch dates with other dudes?"

I was a little taken aback.

"What?"

"Don't play with me! Why the fuck you entertaining other niggas, especially this dusty dude Tate!'

"First off, who are you talking to?" I asked.

"Not now yo, what I tell you about taking to him?"

"It wasn't even like that-"

"So what the fuck was it then?" he screamed.

"You need to calm down." "No I'm not calming down, I haven't talked to that crazy bitch since you told me not to so why the fuck you went against what I told you specifically not to do?"

"Calvin, if you lis-"

"I really don't want to hear shit else you have to say, get out of my car." I looked at him like he was crazy.

"Fuck you Calvin!" I climbed out and slammed the door. I'm not sure what just happened or how it started, all I know is I'm pissed off!

Walk Away

Kelsey

This day has been hell on earth; I don't even know why I agreed to come to school today. I should've stayed my ass home.

My mind was everywhere but on my class. Calvin's little rant had me fuming still and being in the same vicinity as him made my anger heighten.

"Kelsey, are you okay?" my English teacher asked me as I packed up my things.

"Yes, I'm fine." I flashed a fake smile.

"Okay, remember the quiz later in the week."

I nodded and walked out into the hallway. As soon as I was out of view, I rolled my eyes. All in the same breath you're asking me if I'm okay, you put more stress on me. Does that make sense?

The hallway was quiet which meant I was late to my next class. I shrugged it off and walked towards my locker.

"Can we talk?" I turned to the direction in which Calvin's voice was coming from.

"No." I turned to face my locker again, this time I pulled out my coat. I couldn't stay here any longer, not in the state I was in.

"Please?"

I looked at him again. He stood in front of me looking like a lost puppy, that only made me angry again. Now he wants sympathy, leeway? Where was mine?

"Humph!" I put on my coat and slammed the locker's door, I walked away from him but he gently pulled at my arm. I snatched away.

"Now you want to fucking talk? When I tried to have an adult conversation with your ass you kicked me out your car, now you want to talk? Let's talk then, dumb ass! I wasn't on any form of a date. I was having coffee alone, reading, when I was approached by Tate. He apologized and that was the end of our discussion. I didn't even want that much but before, I, your girlfriend could tell you what happened, you believed one of your illiterate ass friends over me. Now you want to talk? You think you could kick me out like I was some side bitch and then expect me to want to talk, no talking doesn't mean shit anymore and you proved that!"

"Ba-" he pulled at my arm.

I quickly snatched away, "Shut the fuck up with that baby shit! Was I your baby when you tried to accuse me of dating someone other than you? No, I wasn't your baby then." He stood there not really processing all that I was saying.

I've never been big on cursing, but this, this called for it. His mouth formed like he was trying to speak but he couldn't. I put him to shame.

Calvin

I sat on my bed scrolling through Kelsey's Instagram. I already know I fucked up. I could've handled it differently. I know and I think that's what fucking with me now.

Just the idea and thought of Kelsey entertaining that corny nigga put me in a place I couldn't describe. I wasn't trying to hear anything. She didn't get it because she didn't have to deal with the worrying another dude coming up to her and saying the right thing to swoop her up and take her from me.

I could hear a light tap at my door.

"Baby, you don't want to eat?"

"I'm good."

She walked further in and sat next to me. "Tell me what's wrong, baby."

"I messed up." I held my head down.

"What happened?"

I explained to her what went down.

"That's not right, you should've at least listened before letting anger take over you. We've talked about that."

"I know, so how do I fix it?"

"As hard as this may be you have to wait and give her time." I sighed.

She picked my face up and kissed my forehead.

"She'll come around papa." She hopped off of my bed and walked down towards the door.

"Come and eat." She walked out and closed the door.

I had to just face the facts. I messed up and there was not much I can do about it this time but wait.

Make Up to Break Up

Kelsey

I lay on my bed clutching my phone tightly. I was trying so hard not to call Calvin and tell him how badly I wanted him to just kiss me.

It had been exactly six days since I'd spoken to him and to be honest I missed my baby.

For the hundredth time I went to his number but instead of exiting out, I decided to call him.

It rang and rang and then he answered.

"Hello." His voice was so deep and sexy when he first woke up.

"Hey, umm can we meet and talk?"

"Are you going to try to fuck me up?"

I giggled lightly and shook my head.

"No, I'm cool."

"Alright, I'll meet you at the pizzeria by your house in 15 minutes."

"Okay I'll see you soon." I hung up and bounced off of my bed. I did a little dance. I honestly have missed him, his lips, his touch and his scent.

I'd kept my feelings stale in front of him, but he knew how I was feeling on the inside. I quickly got dressed, throwing on some leggings his sweatshirt and a pair of Uggs.

I grabbed my phone and walked downstairs. My father was in the kitchen and my mom was curled up on the couch asleep.

I walked towards my dad.

"Daddy, are we still going to the Knicks basketball game?"

He smiled. "You know it baby girl, court side."

I honestly hated basketball but my father loved it and if it made his day for me sit around and watch big fine sweaty men run up and down the court then I was game.

"I'll be back though."

"Going to meet up with Calvin?"

I nodded.

"Tell that nigga he has one more time to mess up and I'm paying him a visit." He put his protein shake in the fridge as if he didn't just threaten someone.

"Daddy, calm down."

"I'm just saying, you know how I get down." When my father was mad or agitated his Harlem accent would get heavy.

"Okay, I'm leaving now." I kissed his cheek. "Tell Mommy where I went when she wakes up."

He nodded.

"Wait Daddy, can I take your Porsche?"

"Yeah, I don't care. It has better traction anyway for that snow."

I nodded and walked out the door.

The ride to the pizzeria was pretty short and I was thankful because I wasn't in the mood for a lot of driving. I parked and walked towards the entrance of the pizzeria, but not before catching a glimpse of my baby on his phone.

Lord he's fine.

I finally walked in and sat in front of him.

"Hey."

He looked up from his phone as I slid in the booth. "What's up?" he spoke coolly. He turned his phone face down and looked at me.

Just then the pizza came out.

"How'd you know I only like cheese baked lightly?"

"Even though you're mad at me, you're still my girl. I remember everything."

I tried to hide my smile. "Calvin, you really took me to a place I've never been before. How could you accuse me of talking to someone else?"

He sighed and then paused for a minute. "I fucked up baby and I know that. I should've never thought like that, I'm just, just afraid of losing my baby quicker than I'm already expecting."

"What are you talking about?"

"When we graduate Ma, there's no telling what's going to happen. We're going to have so much already going on; imagine how it's going to be trying to maintain long distance?"

"Calvin, you have to trust that I'm never going anywhere regardless of our distance. I just wish you'd trust me more."

He blew out a breath. "It's me baby, not you, I trust you."

"Well, if you trust me then why didn't you take for granted that I did the right thing, why'd you believe your corny ass friend before me?"

"I wasn't thinking Kelsey; I know I'm wrong now."

"As long as you're admitting your wrong, I'm good.

He grinned. "So do I have my baby back?"

I smiled lightly, "I guess."

"Can I have a kiss?" He asked.

"Do you deserve one?" I asked.

"Yeah, I think I do." He said cockily.

"Oh really?" I asked while raising my eyebrow.

He leaned over and kissed me.

"Hmm," I moaned against his lips. He finally let go and sat back down.

"Why Calvin, why must you be extra?"

"What?" He asked innocently.

"Uh-huh, you know what?"

He smiled.

We ate and then he insisted on walking me to my car. "Oh shit, my baby's pushing a Porsche. You so popping!"

"You're so silly, it's my dad's." I reached to open the door but he stopped me.

"Where's my kiss?" I smiled and kissed his lips.

He grabbed my waist and took a handful of my butt.

"I missed doing that." He grunted.

"Get off of me boy." I tried to push him off but it was no use.

"You know you missed it too."

I smiled because deep down inside I did.

We stayed with his arms wrapped around my waist and my

hand around his neck for a while.

"Baby, I promised myself I wouldn't allow myself to be in one of those annoying ass relationships where they make up and breakup every five minutes, now look at us."

"I mean real relationships have problems babe, nothing's perfect."

"I guess."

"You didn't think I was letting you go that fast, ugly?" He playfully mushed my head.

"Boy, you better watch those hands."

"Yeah whatever, take your ass home. It's about to get bad out here." He opened my door and then leaned in.

"I love you Ma."

I smiled and could instantly feel my cheeks heat up.

"I love you more." We kissed again and then went our separate ways.

That's my baby and I'll love him regardless, just like he loves me.

Happy Birthday

Kelsey

I looked in the mirror and admired my look for tonight. It was in fact my birthday and I must admit, I looked good.

My aunt had done the unthinkable and gotten me a custom Alexander McQueen piece. It showcased my curves all while shielding some of the unflattering parts of my body.

I sat on the edge of my bed and closed the clasp on each of my heels.

"Little girl, do you not see the time?" My Aunt had agreed to drive me to the place where my birthday dinner would be held, only after my mom insisted on leaving ahead of me. She's been driving me crazy.

"I'm coming!" I stood up. She walked in and gasped loudly.

"Look at you!" She yelled.

I smiled lightly and walked towards her. "I'm trying to be happy Auntie, but I'm a bit upset."

"Why?" she asked while walking towards the front door.

"I still haven't heard from Cal, and it's pissing me off."

"Babygirl it's your day, don't let anything get in the way of that."

"You're right." I smiled and walked ahead of her.

An all-black Ferrari adorned my driveway and I was happy

that my parents fulfilled my request. I've been dying to ride around in one.

The restaurant is in the city so it took us some time to get there but when we finally did I was completely blown away. The restaurant was super dope and what made it even better was the fact that my family covered every inch of the room.

"Guys thank you so much for putting this together, it's beautiful." I beamed. I looked around the room admiring the decorations. All of my family surrounded the small room at Sugar Factory.

"Princess, you deserve this." my father spoke sincerely. I ran towards him and kissed his cheek lightly.

"I love you Daddy with my heart."

I could hear the flashing of cameras and the faint aww's.

"Mommy, you too." I kissed her sweetly and wiped the tears from under my eyes. I'm not sure why I'm so emotional today. I'm guessing it was the idea of being 18 that was messing with me.

I pulled away and sat at the table. I joked around with my cousins and Aria for some time while we waited for the food. When the food finally came out everyone was in their very own world. I glanced down at my phone noticing Calvin hadn't texted me yet. I was pretty annoyed, but I didn't let it show. I just turned my phone over and joined in on Dwayne and Aria's conversation.

"Excuse me; I'd like to propose a toast." I looked over at my dad who held the glass of Champagne outward. He cleared his throat. "I just want to say to my Princess that I'm proud of the woman you're becoming. You're my everything, just know that KK.

You'll always be daddy's princess, regardless the age. "

I blew him a kiss and then my mom stood up and said a couple of words. That's what got the tears flowing. Lord knows how close my mom and I are.

"Now let's sing Happy Birthday, enough of the tears."

Everyone wiped their eyes and focused their attention to the waitresses. Some held my cake and others held sparklers. They began to sing but then stopped mid-song. I looked up and gasped loudly; my hands covered my mouth as I tried to calm myself down. My baby was here.

All of my family began to aww while I wrapped my arms around his waist.

"Why you crying?" He whispered to me.

"You came!"

"You thought I was going to miss this, baby?"

I looked in his eyes and smiled.

Everyone returned to their seats and ate some cake.

"I want to kiss you so bad right now." I said while staring at him.

He looked back at the table and then at me, "Come with me." I looked at him, completely ignoring everyone else in the room.

"Let's go." We both stood up and walked towards the door.

Nobody paid much attention to us so we slipped out easily.

Calvin wrapped his arms around my waist bringing my ear close to his lips. "You look good babe."

I shivered under his touch, "Thank you, you do too." For some reason I felt nervous like we just met or something.

He nibbled on my ear.

"Babe, I thought you were in Cali."

"I was but I left early, you know I couldn't have missed this for the world."

I smiled and turned to face him. I laid a sweet supple kiss on his lips.

I kissed him again, "Love you." I pecked his lips lightly but that wasn't enough for him.

He pulled me by my waist and held me tight. His tongue massaged mine leaving the minty scent of his breath on my lips. We stayed like this until we heard the clearing of a throat.

A woman, I'm guessing a waitress, gave us a pointed look. She looked me up and down and then did the same to Calvin.

I looked at her the same way and Calvin pulled my hand. "Let's go to my car Mayweather."

I giggled lightly before following behind him.

The cool breeze felt good.

"Stay here."

He reached in the back of his car pulling out a large box and a small gift bag. "Here, open this before we go back in there. I don't want everyone to see." He handed me the small bag.

I looked at him and smiled and then back at the bag.

I began to unravel the tissue paper, "Calvin, who wrapped this?" I stopped for a minute.

"Me, I didn't have time to have someone else do it."

I smiled and went back to opening the gift. When my fingertips grazed the cool steel I already knew what it was.

I pulled it out and nearly passed out.

A beautiful diamond encrusted necklace along with a tennis bracelet came into view.

"Baby," I spoke slowly.

He looked at me and smiled. "You like it?" He asked.

"I love it baby." I grabbed his face and kissed his lips.

"Let me put it on you."

I turned while he adjusted the chain around my neck.

I turned to face him again.

"Will it be bad if I left my own party and went with my baby instead?" I asked.

"As good as that sounds Ma, your uncle and pops are not about to kill me." I laughed lightly.

"Your right." We walked hand and hand back into the restaurant.

No one can take this moment from me, no one.

Getaway

Calvin

"Pops, what is it?" I jogged down the stairs.

"Why your ass never have a shirt on?" he asked.

I sucked my teeth.

"What?" I walked further in the living room only to see Kelsey, Aria and Dwayne. All of our parents sat across from them. I scrunched my eyes up in confusion.

"What y'all doing here?" I asked, sitting next to Kelsey.

"I don't know." she said sweetly. From the corner of my eye I could see her staring at me biting that bottom lip. I put my hand on her thigh but moved it when I saw how my father and her father looked at me.

My mom cleared her throat and started to talk, "We couldn't be any more proud of all of you as we are now, so we wanted to give you guys something." They each handed us an envelope.

I cracked the seal ready to open it up but before I could finish, they stopped me.

"On three I want y'all to open it." Aria's father said.

"1, 2, 3" We all opened it and I nearly passed out.

"I can't believe this; we're going to Turks and Caicos!" Kelsey yelled.

"Yes God! Now I have to go shopping!" Aria's dramatic ass yelled.

"Well you guys better hurry. You're leaving tomorrow night." Kelsey's father said.

I looked over at Dwayne. We looked at the girls and smirked, the stuff I was thinking about should be illegal.

"Don't make that face fresh ass, there will be supervision. You may not see them but they're there." my mother said.

We each thanked our parents. I was ready to thank God! I'm going to the most beautiful place on the planet with the sexiest girl alive, life couldn't get any better.

Kelsey

"Ouch Mommy!" I yelled. She was sewing my hair in all while killing me at the same time.

"Sorry baby, you're almost done." I scrolled down my newsfeed. Calvin was a few people's MCM. Now I could be petty and report each of their pages, but I'm cool. They can look as long as they don't touch.

"So when is our flight leaving again Mommy?"

"7 am."

"I'm so excited; I must've called Aria thousands of times."

She grinned and looked at me through the mirror. "You deserve it, all done."

I smiled and kissed her cheek. "I'm going upstairs to finish packing." I kissed her cheek once more and walked towards my bedroom. I pulled out the outfit I was going to wear there and laid it on my couch.

I grabbed my phone off of my bed and called Calvin.

"Yo?" he answered.

I rolled my eyes. I hated when he answered the phone like that. "What are you doing?" I asked.

"Packing some more of my stuff."

I tied my scarf on my head and closed my suitcase, "That's exactly what I'm doing now, let's match babe."

"Why you always want us matching?" he asked, slightly amused.

"It's cute." I got in my bed.

"Nah, that's what you and Aria do, not me."

I sucked my teeth, "Please baby!" I whined.

"Fine, under one condition."

"What?"

"Phone sex."

I smiled and turned off my lamp, "Fine."

The next day we were all ready to go. Calvin's hands were wrapped around my waist as we waited for our car to pick us up.

"Give me kiss." he spoke huskily.

I reached up and gave him a quick peck.

"Y'all, the car is here." Aria yelled. Our parents arranged for us to have a car service pick us up and drop us off.

I started to walk towards her and Dwayne while Calvin followed behind me.

Hours later, we were finally there. The Escalade rode through the streets of Turk. I took my phone out and captured a couple of pictures. I switched it over to a video and put the camera on Aria and Dwayne.

And then Calvin.

"Baby?"

He looked towards my phone and smiled.

The video ended and I slid my phone into my purse.

"I'm so excited baby." I leaned into Calvin's side.

"I can tell, your energetic ass hasn't stop talking!"

I hit him playfully. "Shut up! I'm excited for the beach." I said. I was beyond ready to soak up some sun.

"Nah babe, I'm ready to eat. I heard food here is bomb."

"Hmm."

We came to a complete stop.

"Your here" the driver said.

I looked at our Villa in amazement, it was beyond beautiful. This vacation is going to be the absolute best. I was in paradise with my baby.

"Are you sure it's not too much?" I asked Aria as I rubbed some Shea lotion on my legs.

We were getting ready to go to the beach so I decided to wear this black fringed bathing suit and a sheer t-shirt cover-up from Moschino. It fit my body perfectly but I was a little apprehensive when it came down to showcasing my thighs.

I pushed those feelings to the side and stood up to walk towards our private beach.

Aria followed behind me. The guys were already on the beach tossing a football back and forth.

"God is so good." I could hear Aria whisper. Her eyes were glued to Dwayne.

"Yes he is," I said to myself. I watched as Calvin's muscles flexed while he ran up and down the beach.

He turned his attention to me and stopped for a minute. His mouth was ajar. He tapped Dwayne's shoulder, signaling for him to look in our direction.

"Girl, look how they're looking at us." Aria said through

clenched teeth.

"I know right." I said low.

They started to walk towards us. Dwayne grabbed Aria and ran off.

Calvin stood staring at me. He walked around me and looked me up and down.

"Babe, why are you looking at me like that?" I was beginning to feel weird under his glare.

"Damn Ma." I smiled trying to hide my cheeks that were red from blushing.

He stood behind me and wrapped his arms around my waist.

I could feel him harden as soon as my butt came in contact with his rod.

"I'm trying so hard baby to respect your wishes, but you're not making it easy." He whispered in my ear. His hands caressed my thighs.

"I might give you what you've been wanting." I said low. You know when you say something so quickly that you didn't have enough time to gather your thoughts.

"Huh?" he asked while rubbing my arm up and down.

I stopped and thought about what I was going to say next. I couldn't cover up this one.

"I said maybe I'll give you what you want."

"Don't play with me baby." he growled.

"I'll put it in your life." I pulled away from him and hit his chest.

"Get away from me."

He laughed lightly. "Don't act like you're not horny."

On the inside I wanted him just as bad as he wanted me. I was starting to have feelings I'd never experienced towards sex. I was horny but I'll never let him know that.

"Whatever, let's go in the water." I pulled his arm.

"Aren't you wet enough?"

"You're so nasty, I swear!" I yelled.

I could hear him laugh lightly.

I'm hoping I leave here in the way I came, but I'm making no promises.

Aria

The sun began to set giving us a perfect view. I laid my head on Dwayne's chest.

"I love you baby." I said. We hadn't said anything remotely close to I love you and it felt good to share that with him.

"I love you too." he said low. I ran my hands up and down his chest.

"Can I be honest with you baby?"

"Yeah."

"I want you to be my first."

He perked up, "You want me to take your virginity?" He asked. He was trying to convince himself.

"Yeah." I believed I'm ready to take that step. He stood and we walked back towards the Villa.

I could feel my palms sweat profusely, I can't believe I'm really about to do this.

Calvin

"Walk slowly Ma." I recorded Kelsey as she walked up the three short steps to our Villa.

"Why are you so nasty?" she asked. Like I said before, I'm horny and it feels like forever since we did anything.

Her thick ass in that bathing suit was working wonders, I mean damn. Her thighs were thick but still nice and toned. Her ass was on an island by its self, it was just so nice and round. The way she walked was enough to drive a nigga crazy.

We walked further into the villa, "I'm hungry babe." Kelsey whined.

"Let's go out then."

She smiled, "Go tell Dwayne and Aria while I get ready."

I nodded and jogged up the stairs. I knocked a couple of times before he finally opened the door.

"Damn, how long I have to wait?"

"Man whatever, what you need?" he said rushing me.

"Nothing, me and Kelsey about to grab something to eat, y'all want to come?"

He looked back behind the door and then at me. "Nah, we cool."

I looked at him, "What y'all about to do in here?"

He pushed me back. "Man, mind your business." He closed the

door.

I laughed, "Use protection!" I yelled. I walked back towards the bedroom Kelsey and I were sharing. We weren't supposed to be sharing one, but hey we could break a rule or two.

I could hear the shower running and her music playing. I walked in.

"Baby?" I called out to her.

"Yeah?" She answered.

"I love you, you know that?"

She giggled lightly, "I love you too, but where's this coming from? You stole another pair of my panties?"

I honestly thought she forgot about that.

"Nah, I can't just say I love my girl?"

"That's so sweet baby, I love you more. Now go so I can get ready."

"Fine, I'm going to come shower with you. You know, to save time." I was expecting her to say no but she didn't say anything.

I took that as a yes. I undressed and hopped in behind her. I'd had chances to explore her body, but I must say, I can process it better this way. I took her wash rag from her and began to wipe her down slowly, she looked at me innocently.

Her hands traveled down my chest exploring my body.

I did the same to her. "Turn around." I said firmly. She did as I asked. I stood behind her and closed the gap between us.

"You're so fucking beautiful." I could feel her shiver under my touch.

I kissed her neck and she began to moan. She turned to face

me and began to kiss me aggressively. Her hands began to glide down from my chest to my lower half. Her hands wrapped around me tightly. To be honest, I wasn't expecting her to do anything. I thought it would be all me. She kissed down from my stomach to the tip.

"What you doing Ma?" I couldn't even think straight.

She started to swirl her tongue around the head. She took all of me in her mouth. I held her head as she put more and more of me in her mouth.

My eyes rolled back.

"Damn" was all I could say. She picked up the pace sending me over the edge.

"Shit babe move." I could feel myself about to release. She moved to the side.

Without hesitation I picked her up and put her up against wall. Her legs rested on my shoulders.

This definitely isn't over; she didn't know what she started.

Kelsey

I flipped my hair over my shoulder. I decided to straighten it after taking that well needed shower.

I was feeling so good that I decided to wear heels. Calvin held my hand tightly as we walked past the busy restaurants. Caribbean music spilled into the streets as we enjoyed the scenery.

"Taste this." I put the pineapple ice cream to his lips.

"I'm good."

I rolled my eyes. "Please baby?" I pouted.

"No, take that nasty shit over there with you."

I laughed lightly at him. "Please?" I whined some more.

"Fine man, give me."

I smiled and he took the come from my hand. He tasted it and looked at me. "It's good." He continued to lick the ice cream, devouring it.

"Calvin! You ate all of my damn ice cream!"

He finished it off and turned to kiss me. Instead I put my hand up, dodging it.

"That's how you want to be?"

I playfully ignored him. I walked ahead of him, pretending to be angry until he came behind me and picked me up.

"Put me down!" I said through laughter.

"Say you love me!"

"Nope!"

He began to tickle my sides. I laughed uncontrollably.

"You want me to put you down?"

"Yes!"

"Give me a kiss." He looked at me like he never looked at me before.

Both of our laughter died down. We kissed and it was almost electric. This is a love I'd never get ever again.

Aria

"I'm sorry; I don't know I just froze up." I closed my pink satin robe and stood up.

I'm not sure what was going on with me, but I know I'm definitely not ready for sex. Dwayne and I were minutes away from going into full throttle, but I choked up, leaving him frustrated.

He may have wanted to keep his frustrations to himself but I knew him all too well.

I could feel his presence behind me. "Baby I keep telling you, it's alright that you weren't ready." He kissed my shoulder.

I wiped the tears from my eyes.

"Stop that Ma."

I nodded and wiped the brim of my eyes. "Can we cuddle?" I asked. Dwayne was literally my big teddy bear. To others he may have been intimidating, but to me he's my baby.

"C'mon." He pulled me to him and kissed my cheek.

I climbed in the bed and he did the same. All that could be heard was the ceiling fan and the waves crashing into the sand, it was all so soothing.

"Can I tell you something?" I said low.

"Hmm?" he answered.

"I got accepted into Rutgers."

I could feel that the grip he had on me got tighter. "But I'm coming with you to UCLA."

"No."

I looked up at him, "Why?" I asked.

"I don't want you to come because of me, come because of you."

I smiled to myself. "I love you." I kissed his chest and laid my head on him.

"I love you too, go to sleep. I'm tired." He kissed my head and drifted off.

I've already made up my mind; UCLA is where I wanted to be.

Kelsey

Today was bittersweet. It was our last day here in Turks so we decided to have a small dinner. I pulled my kinky curly mane into a messy bun.

"Babe, what are you wearing?" I asked Calvin.

"Grey everything." He came out with a towel wrapped around his waist.

I looked at him through the mirror and rolled my eyes. I silently thanked God for allowing me to hide what I'm really thinking.

I stood up and looked in the full length mirror.

"I like that dress." He pulled his shirt over his head.

"Thank you, I was going to change though." I felt this dress was a little too much and to avoid panty lines I had to wear thongs and they were annoying me.

"Nah, keep that on." He sat on the edge of the bed and laced up his sneakers.

"I heard the food at this place where we're going to is so good."

"I know, I'm mad hungry."

I grabbed my phone and my selfie stick. "Baby, let's take pictures."

He stood up and sucked his teeth. "Your ass always want to

take a picture, come on."

I smiled and positioned the stick. I stood in front of him and he wrapped his arms around my waist. We took a couple of pictures; one in particular was my favorite. His arms were wrapped securely around me and we both put on a mean mug.

"We look good together." I said to myself while going through the pictures.

"Let's go." Calvin walked ahead of me towards the bedroom door and I walked in front of him.

"Yo, you got a fatty."

I giggled to myself. "Stop being so nasty." I could hear him behind me.

"It's not nasty baby, it's the truth."

I rolled my eyes and walked towards the living room.

"Y'all, I wish we could stay here forever." Calvin said lowly.

After dinner we came back to the Villa and decided to relax on the private beach.

The entire night at dinner Calvin and I just soaked in one another's company barely talking about what we'll do after we leave this beautiful place.

"I know it's like paradise here." I played with the sand and lay on Calvin's chest.

"I'm trying to process how close we are to being in college." I said while taking a sip of my Piña Colada.

"Word, it feels like we just started school." Calvin said while playing in my hair.

We all looked at the sunset taking in its beauty. I looked at

Calvin who was focused on the waves crashing onto the sand.

I'm not sure what it was, but at that moment I felt something rare like confirmation for something and I think I knew just what that feeling confirmed.

"Let's go to the room." I whispered to Calvin.

"Alright." He got up and I followed. We told Aria and Dwayne that we were going to our room and walked into the Villa.

I've never felt this sure about something ever in my life.

Calvin

"I'll be back; I'm going to go get ready for bed." Kelsey said.

I nodded and walked towards the bed. I stripped down to my boxers and lay under the covers.

A few minutes later, my baby came out in little to no clothes. My jaw hit the floor when I saw what she was wearing. I couldn't help but stare.

"What, you don't like it?" She asked.

"Nah you, you look good." She had me stuttering and shit.

"Thank you." She looked away and bit her bottom lip.

"But you're not sleeping in that right?" Truth be told, I was sexually frustrated and I just know that I wouldn't be able to take her lying next to me in that sexy lingerie.

She walked toward me and stood in between my legs. By nature my hands went straight to her ass.

We stared at each other intently. She parted her lips to speak, but I didn't allow her. I just kissed her.

My lips went from her neck to her lips. I picked her up and laid her on the bed. I kissed from her thighs to her stomach. I stopped to admire her beauty. I'm beyond lucky. I mean to know I'm getting what nobody else had the opportunity to get makes me feel like I'm a King or some shit.

"You good babe?" I asked her for reassurance.

"Yeah, I'm fine." she said softly. I kissed her inner thighs, making my way up towards her middle. I kissed her clit lightly and I was driving her crazy. I blew on it and then attacked it like I was eating my last meal.

Her hands rubbed on my head, slightly pushing me more into her.

I put my finger in her gently.

"Sss" she hissed. I began working my fingers in and out of her all while applying pressure to her clit.

She bucked her hips a little.

"How you feeling?" I asked her.

"I'm o-okay." She began to moan and buck her hips again.

I knew she was ready just by that sudden movement.

I got up from the bed and reached for my bag. I took a condom out and put it on me. I lay on top of her and licked the top of her breast; I toyed with her right nipple while she moaned. I used my knees to separate her legs they wrapped around my waist almost instantly. I slid into her gently and slowly. She gasped and dug her nails into my back. I stared at her all while doing so, her eyes began to water and I kissed away the salty tears that fell down.

"I love you, with everything in me, you hear me?" I asked as I gave her low deep strokes, giving her time to adjust to me.

Her eyes closed as she pulled me closer to her. "I love you too," she said, barely audible. I kissed her as I gave her all of me.

Tonight I did what a lot of dudes my age never experienced. I didn't just fuck, as corny as this sounds, I made love to someone I'm deeply in love with.

Goodbye?

Omniscient

Some storage bins and boxes filled the backseat of his Jeep. Today was the day that they'd been mentally preparing themselves for all summer. She tried to keep the tears from falling, but the more stuff he packed the more she felt the burning sensation coming from her eyes.

"Sweetie, are you fine?" Calvin's mother asked.

All she could was nod, she was too afraid to speak.

Calvin waved her over. He, too, was feeling the sadness.

He watched as she walked over towards him somberly.

As soon as she was able to fall into his arms she did just that, letting the tears soak his crisp white t-shirt.

"C'mon Ma, don't do this." He tried his best to console her but it was like she couldn't stop. He held her close as she held him closer.

"Look at me." Calvin instructed her.

She finally looked up, her face wet from the tears. With the pads of his thumb, he wiped her face clean.

Kelsey looked up but then looked away.

"I'm going to love you regardless." He kissed her forehead.

"I'm going to miss you so much." She began to cry again.

"C'mon, you going to make me cry." He did everything in his power to calm her down.

In public, he played hard ass but in private he cried like a baby. I mean breaking up with your first love isn't easy at all. Due to them being so far away from each other, they decided to call it quits. With them being unfamiliar with their schools they thought long distance wasn't something they could partake in. Football and Education needed to be their main focus.

"I'm sorry." she said softly.

"Look at me." He took her chin between his fingers.

She looked in his eyes and nearly shivered from the intensity that she saw.

"I'm going to be here to support you regardless of anything broken up or not, you gave me something I'll probably never get again."

"And you want me to stop crying?" She lightly giggled and wiped the excess tears from her face.

Even after spending the entire summer together, including their trip to Turks and Caicos, it still felt like they didn't spend enough time together.

"As soon as I get off the plane, I'll call you." Kelsey nodded.

"And just because we aren't together, just know I always got you just like you have me." As soon as those words left Calvin's lips he knew this wasn't going to be easy.

"I'm never going to forget you Calvin, I love you so much." She clung to him tightly.

"I love you too baby." On the inside Calvin's heart was just as twisted and tangled as Kelsey's.

"Come here ugly."

She sucked her teeth and rolled her eyes jokingly. As soon as their lips met, it was almost like they couldn't stop. His hands groped every curve while their tongues went into action.

It took a couple of clearing of throats for is them to separate.

"Damn." Calvin spoke while caressing her cheek.

"Calvin baby, let's not miss your flight." Calvin's mother's soft voice cooed.

He looked back at his mother and then at Kelsey.

"I'm guessing you have to go." Her voice was soft and mellow like.

"Yeah," he answered. His pitch matched hers perfectly. Their fingers were intertwined, squeezing the life out of each other's hands.

At the exact same time they parted their mouths to speak but no words seemed to come out.

A small eerie feel lingered between the two.

"Be good to yourself." Calvin bent down and laid a kiss on Kelsey's forehead.

Calvin needed to walk away before he started crying like a little bitch in front of her.

"Bye baby girl." Mr. and Mrs. Powers yelled while getting into the Jeep.

Wanting one more glance, Calvin turned around and smiled slightly, she did the same.

As she watched the car pull off she could literally feel a piece of her soul leaving her. With all the energy she had left, she got on her car and went straight home.

You can call it young puppy love or dumb love but whatever it was, it was real and deeper than what anyone will ever know.

Kelsey

I packed the last of my bags. I was excited and drained at the same time.

I spent all of last night with my mind on Calvin. This'll be something I feel I truly will never get over. He had a piece of me that I wasn't sure whether I was willing to give away to just anybody. That's just how it had to be for now.

"Baby girl let's get going!" my father yelled

"Okay Daddy, I'm almost done." I pulled my suitcase towards the entrance of my room and looked around noticing how bare it appeared.

All that was left was a couple of awards and pictures. I couldn't help but smile to myself

A new journey is beginning for me and it's time to embrace it.

Shuffling down the stairs with my last and final suitcase, I couldn't help but notice Aria standing in the doorway.

"You're finally ready, God!" She fanned herself as if the heat was too much for her.

"Good another four years with your dramatic ass." I joked.

That's right! Aria decided to come to the city with me and attend Columbia as well.

Our parents set us up at this Trendy loft in Manhattan and I was beyond ready to see it.

"You love me!" She yelled while walking to the Sprinter my dad rented out for us all to take to the city.

Ready wasn't the word though, Calvin would be wedged in my brain. my main focus needs to be on my education and that's exactly where it's going to be. Hopefully, just hopefully, I can find someone as special as Calvin.

Made in the USA
Middletown, DE
25 May 2021